FIRST WITCH

THE AWAKENING SERIES - BOOK TWO

JANE HINCHEY

BAYWOLF PRESS
BP
BAYWOLF PRESS

ABOUT THIS BOOK

If discovering you come from a long line of witches wasn't left-field enough, Georgia soon learns that she has a target on her back in the form of a witch hunter. Should be easy enough to deal with considering her new vampire status, but she soon discovers she'd misjudged the hunter, and he is a greater foe than she'd ever imagined.

When the hunter does the unthinkable and possesses the body of her boyfriend in an effort to take down Georgia's entire coven, things get even more complicated. She can't defeat the one she fears the most without harming the one she loves.

Stuck between a rock and a hard place Georgia has to rely on her wits and mysteriously changing magic to save herself and everyone she holds dear... or die trying.

AUTHOR'S NOTE

Hey! Welcome to the weird and wacky world of my imagination! I hope you enjoy your time here.

If you love your supernatural adventures with heat and sizzle, then you're going to enjoy the journey ahead — at least, I think you will.

Fair warning, most of my books are cozy mysteries. This is definitely not one of those books. While there is mystery, intrigue, and suspense, there is also swearing, violence and sex. If this your jam, read on. If not, one of my cozy mysteries may suit you better.

No matter your preference, I'd love to connect with you.

Sign up for my newsletter: https:// JaneHinchey.com/subscribe

Join my VIP Reader Group: www.JaneHinchey.com/LittleDevils

Ready to get started?
I'll see you on the other side!

xoxo

Jane

A wave of energy flooded the air, warping, twisting, turning, an invisible tsunami ripping through time and space. Around the globe it traveled, never losing pace, undetected by some. Others felt it pass through them. It left them reeling in its wake, shaken, energized...aware.

His eyes flickered open.

"Finally." His voice was hoarse from disuse. Slowly he rose, muscles stiff, blood pooled unmoving in his veins. Each movement was excruciating. The only sound in the dark room was his breath as he sucked air into disused lungs.

It took an age, but eventually, he was on his feet, shuffling to the cupboard across the room. Dust covered the floor, motes rising up and dancing in the air as he dragged himself forward. With a slight groan, he leaned and opened the cupboard, pulling a metal flask from its depths, twisting the lid, and raising it to his lips, gulping. The contents spilled over his chin and down his bare chest, the liquid cutting through the layer of grime covering him to reveal a glimpse of the symbols that marked his skin.

"Aaaah. Better." Already he could feel the ambrosia reviving him—his dried flesh became supple once more, the blood circulating through his veins, sluggish at first, soon picking up speed, bringing color and life to his body. Moving easier now, he crossed the room and flicked the light switch. A single bulb dangled from the ceiling, casting the room in a yellow glow. His tattoos itched, and he absently brushed his palm over them, soothing the ache. Soon, he promised them. Soon.

A door stood ajar, its paint peeling. With renewed vigor, he pushed the door open, reaching in to flick on that light too. The bathroom was old, tiles falling from the walls, rust winning the battle with enamel in the old tub. The shower curtain had long since rotted away; now flakes of plastic scattered across the floor, crumbling into dust beneath his feet.

With fingers that trembled ever so slightly, he turned on the tap, a grunt of satisfaction when hot water coughed and spluttered through the shower, settling into a steady stream. Stepping beneath the spray, he sucked in a breath as the water pummeled his skin like fine needles. It was always like this. The awakening.

Clean, naked, and dripping, he stood in front of the bathroom mirror, watching as his sunken face continued to fill out, his cheeks no longer hollow, his eyes no longer deep in their sockets. He raised a hand, traced his jaw with fingers that were no longer old and wrinkled. He was back. It was time.

He stopped a young boy no more than thirteen years old in the street.

"What time is it?" he demanded, gripping the boy's wrist as he would have moved on past.

"Hey. Let go," the boy protested, tugging on his arm. Then he looked into the man's eyes and froze, unblinking.

"What time is it?" the man asked again.

"Two o'clock." the boy replied.

"Date?"

"The first of October."

"Year?"

"Two thousand and sixteen."

"Go. Remember nothing."

The boy continued on his way, unaware of what had just transpired, a grin on his face and a spring in his step as he spied his friends waiting for him in front of the cinema.

The man continued to stand on the sidewalk, raising his face to the sky as dark clouds began to gather overhead. A boom of thunder rattled windows. The man smiled.

"I'm coming for you, witch."

SHE SHOULD HAVE BEEN PREPPING Zak's dining table. It was ready for its first coat of stain. Yet here she stood, the figurine she'd just carved clasped tightly in her hand, breath heaving in her lungs, horror creeping up and tapping her on the shoulder. What had she done?

Something was wrong. Georgia knew it on a deep, intrinsic level. What it was, exactly, she couldn't put her finger on, but she could feel it, like a darkness creeping into her soul, slithering through her veins, darkening her, changing her. And it scared the absolute shit out of her.

Ever since the showdown with Marius, where

she'd ripped Veronica's heart from her chest, it had niggled at her. The guilt. The knowledge that when she'd become a vampire, she'd changed in ways she'd never anticipated. To take the life of another? The idea was abhorrent to her, yet she'd launched at Veronica, and, fueled by rage, she'd sunk her hand into the woman's chest, unrepentant in her actions, with no hesitation. Veronica had never physically harmed her. Oh yes, the woman had been a first-class bitch and had been involved in the torture she'd suffered at the hands of Marius. Did she deserve to die? At the time, Georgia had thought so. Now, weeks later, she wasn't so sure.

Tearing her unseeing eyes from the table back to the figurine in her hand, she trembled, a shudder rippling through her. It was a monster. Jaws open wide, long teeth protruding from the mouth, face contorted, clawed hands clutching...a heart. The face was almost unrecognizable. Almost. But Georgia knew who it was. Her. It was her. She was the monster. With a curse, she hurled it at the wall where it fell, rolling to a stop next to the two other identical figurines. She hadn't meant to carve them; she'd returned to her workshop intending to work on Zak's dining table. It was long overdue, yet here she was, the third carving that she didn't remember making.

She glanced outside the open doors. Dawn wasn't far off; she'd best head back. That was another thing that took getting used to. No more daylight. Switching off the lights and locking up the workshop, she checked her beloved farmhouse was secure before jumping in her truck and spinning the tires down the driveway. She arrived at Zak's house within minutes, skidding to a halt with a cloud of dust, killing the engine and the boom of the stereo. Climbing out of the truck, she strode around the back of the house, following the sound of voices. Skye was practicing knife throwing, being cheered on by Zak and his warriors.

"Hey." Noticing her, Zak tugged her in close to his side, dropping a kiss on the top of her head. His warmth reached out and embraced her, weaving around her, making her feel safe...protected.

"How's it going?" She nodded at Skye, who was throwing knives through the air and embedding them in the wooden bull's eye with amazing precision.

"She's good. A natural." Georgia eyed her sweet little sister, noting the change in her too. Gone was the cute, preppy look of pencil skirts, polka dots, and high ponytails, in its place skin-tight black jeans, a black tank, and shit-kicker boots. All that remained of the old Skye was the ponytail.

She rubbed at her head, a headache beginning to pound behind her eyes. Zak frowned down at her.

"Everything okay?"

"Just a headache. I'll be fine." She pulled out of his embrace, giving him a wan smile. "I'm going to head inside, get some sustenance. That should fix me right up." She couldn't bring herself to say blood, that she needed to drink blood. She'd been hiding from him her wavering thoughts on becoming a vampire. It was too late now anyway. There was nothing she could do about it. Once you turned vampire, there was no going back.

"Georgia?" His head tilted to the side, his dark eyes zeroing in on her with laser precision.

"I'm fine," she grumbled, hurrying inside. Heating her mug of blood in the microwave, she stood at the kitchen sink, gazing unseeing into the darkness outside as she sipped. As much as her mind protested her new species status, her body embraced it, the blood reviving her, bringing a flush to her cheeks and a sparkle in her eyes. Yet still, the throbbing in her head continued.

"Better?" Zak pressed in behind her, his arms

sliding around her waist, his mouth at her ear. She nodded, letting her head drop back against his shoulder. Best he didn't know that she was changing, that something terrible was happening to her. Pulling herself together, she plastered on a smile, turning in his embrace and wrapping her arms around his neck.

"Much." She tugged his head down until his mouth was on hers. This was still the same. The electricity, the thrumming of her body, the weakness in her knees, the way she came completely undone when he touched her. Breath hitching, she pressed herself closer, shuddering when he growled, the deep rumble vibrating through her. She didn't protest when he teleported them upstairs to the bedroom they shared, smiled in sultry delight when he tossed her on the bed, and followed her down. Oh yes, this, she didn't mind at all.

CHAPTER
TWO

There's nothing like starting your day with tequila shots. With only slightly blurry vision, she grinned at Eddie. It had been an age since she'd visited the pub across the road from Behind the Times, the shop she and Skye owned.

"Missed you around these parts." He refilled the shot glass, a grin tugging at his lips as she promptly drained it before he'd had a chance to put the bottle down.

"Yeah, been hanging at the farm mostly, waiting on the repairs to the shop." She waved a hand in the general direction of the store across the street. The one that Marius's men had set on fire. He didn't need to know that she'd never be able to work in the shop again, that daylight was now her enemy.

"It's been slow going."

"Insurance. They want to approve every damn little thing. Assholes," she muttered, thinking now of all the phone calls and frustrations they'd endured as the insurance company kept them hanging.

"You're that chick who's living with that Goodwin dude in his mansion." A skinny guy in dirty jeans, a ratty T-shirt, and a baseball cap slid onto the barstool to her left, eyeing her up and down. His tone was accusing. She frowned at him.

"What of it?" She nodded at Eddie, who refilled her glass for the umpteenth time.

"I hear your sister's there too. You both giving it up for him?"

His words skittered along her skin, dirty, unclean. Eddie sucked in a breath. "Hey now, no need for that," he admonished the jerk who thought he knew her, knew Skye. *Loser.* Why did guys always do this? Couldn't she just sit at the bar and get shit-faced drunk without these idiots? Just once. Blowing out a breath, she swiveled on her seat and eyeballed him, her face cold.

"Fuck. Off."

He threw back his head and laughed, then leaned toward her, leering. "I like your spunk. I bet you're a fucking firecracker in the sack. Want to come outside and give this a spin?" He grabbed his crotch.

"Nope." Ignoring him, she turned back to the bar and her drink. Eddie raised a brow at her, surprise on his face. Usually, by now, she'd have punched the guy in the face. Maybe being a vampire had taught her some restraint. Perhaps she just wasn't that bothered by what people thought anymore. She grinned and tossed back the tequila.

"Let's mix it up, Eddie." She pointed to a bottle behind him. "This calls for whiskey."

"You sure?" He turned and reached for the bottle and a fresh glass. Piling ice into the bottom, he poured a double shot.

"Absa-fucking-lutely," she assured him. The tequila had given her a nice buzz, had taken the edge off her angst, although the headache still thrummed behind her eyes. The one she'd been hiding from Zak because, for one, he'd fuss, and two, vampires didn't get headaches. Something was wrong with her.

The jerk seemed content to settle in next to her, snide, rude comments sliding from his small mouth every time Eddie stepped away to serve someone else. Georgia ignored him, didn't really hear what insults he was flinging her way, her mind on other things. It wasn't until he touched her that he brought her full attention back to him. His hand was on her knee, sliding up her thigh. She brought her own hand down on top of his and squeezed. Hard.

"Fuck!" he cried, his bones close to snapping.

"Considering your lowly opinion of me, I'm somewhat surprised that you'd want to touch me, but since you did, here's a newsflash, asshole. Don't. Don't ever touch me. Got it?" She flung his hand away, and he cradled it against his chest, his eyes spitting fire at her. He slugged down his beer, built up his courage, and was in her face, lips inches from hers.

"You're nothing but a filthy whore. I'll do what I want, touch what I want, and you'll fucking love it, bitch!" His breath was fetid, and spit landed on her cheek. *Gross.* Closing her eyes on a weary sigh, she moved before he could draw his next breath, propelling him across the room with a hand around his throat and pinning him to the wall. He was gasping, scratching at her hand, eyes bulging and face turning red. She observed him, head tilted. It would be so easy to snap his worthless neck; even as the thought skittered across her mind, her fingers tightened.

"Hey now, what's going on here?" Rhys's voice was in her ear, calm, cautious. She cast a glance at him over her shoulder, "Oh hey, Rhys. Whatcha doing here?"

"I was hoping for a quiet drink, but I walk in and see this." He nodded at the grip she still had on the loser, his face turning from red to purple. "I think you should let him go, Georgia. I'm sure he's learned his lesson."

"Do you think?" She looked at the loser again, who was nodding his head as best he could, frantic to draw breath. She waited another second, then let go. He doubled over, hands on his knees, sucking in wheezing breaths.

"You fucking bitch!" he spat, still bent over. Rhys stepped up, grabbing the guy by the shirt collar and hauling him to the front door.

"Seriously, dude, you've got no brains. Go home. Sober up. And stop insulting womenfolk."

"Who are you to tell me what to do?"

"I'm the law." That shut him up. Casting a hateful glare at Georgia, he let Rhys shove him outside, grumbling under his breath.

Georgia was back at the bar, sipping on her

whiskey, ignoring the other patrons who'd watched the whole episode unfold and were now staring at her. Rhys slid onto the same stool the loser had occupied and ordered a beer.

"So," he said.

"So," she replied.

"Care to tell me what that was all about?"

"The usual. Some jerk who thinks his tiny pecker is God's gift to women and that I should bow down and worship at his feet, or more precisely—"

"Don't say it!" Rhys cut her off. "I can imagine. Are you okay?"

"Of course. Take more than that pathetic excuse of a man to get to me."

She could feel Rhys's eyes on her.

"What?" She didn't look at him, kept swishing her whiskey in the glass.

"You're sweating," he commented.

"What?" This time she did look at him. He frowned, taking a swig of beer as he continued to study her, the dots of perspiration on her forehead, the flush to her cheeks.

"I didn't think vampires would sweat."

"They don't. Well, not very often. Only after very strenuous activity, and only briefly."

"Then why are you? That little brawl would have

barely got your heart rate up." He reached out and touched a hand to her forehead. "Shit! You've got a fever; you're fucking burning up, Georgia." He placed his beer on the bar and swiveled on his stool. Grabbing her shoulders, he turned her to face him.

"It's probably just the alcohol." She shrugged. Maybe she was sick? At the moment, she didn't care. The tequila and whiskey had done their job of numbing her, numbing her to the worry of the darkness inside.

"I'm calling Zak." He pulled out his phone, but she smacked it out of his hand, wincing when she heard it smash on the floor.

"No. I'm fine. I don't need Zak fussing. So I'm running a little hot, so what? It's fine. I'm fine. Just let me be." She slid off her barstool, pulled a wad of notes out of her back pocket, and slammed them down on the bar, preparing to leave.

"Georgia." Rhys sighed, sliding off his own stool and grabbing her arm. "Don't leave. I'm sorry. Can't we just sit and have a drink together? Like the old days? I've missed you."

His words tore through her, leaving a hole in her heart. She missed him too. He'd been her best friend before Zak had turned her world upside down. Back when things were simple when they'd flirt with the idea of kissing, then back away because their friendship was too important to them. And then everything had changed. *Everything*. Nothing was the same, and she couldn't turn back the clock. Her eyes reflected the agony inside, the bleakness churning through her, the alcohol already burning off and leaving her depressingly sober.

RHYS KNEW HER SO WELL, was so connected to her he could practically feel what she was feeling. He reeled under the emotions pouring from her, warring with each other. Love, happiness, joy, despair, pain, regret. They all fought within her, ripping her to shreds. Then she clamped a lid on them, clamped it on tight, and he felt nothing. She gently moved her arm out of his hold and walked away.

He let her go, a frown on his face. Something was wrong. Every instinct in his body was screaming at him to help her, but to do that, he'd have to go against her wishes, go behind her back. *To Zak*. Their friendship had taken such a beating when she'd turned vampire, and it hadn't fully recovered. He didn't know if it ever would. If he did this, if he interfered, would she forgive him? It was a chance he was prepared to take. To save her.

Georgia drove to the farmhouse, cheeks wet with tears she didn't know she was crying. She couldn't pull Rhys any further into her fucked up world. It was better this way, she told herself over and over. A dozen times, she'd wanted to turn her truck around and go have that drink with him, make plans for the weekend, sit and chat like the old days, back when life was easy and simple. Back when she was human.

Pulling to a stop in her driveway, she killed the engine and sat in the cab, drawing in deep breaths, getting her emotions under control. She forced herself to focus on what she'd gained over what she'd lost. Her sister was happy, healthy, and strong. Skye had settled into her vampire life quickly and clearly loved it. And Zak. She'd met the man of her dreams, her soul mate. They were connected on a million different levels; each one of them had slotted effortlessly into place. He was hers. She was his. Her lips curled, and, feeling better, she jumped out of the truck and headed into the workshop.

Eyeing the dining table that had started to become her nemesis, an idea struck her. Black. She had to paint it black with a blood-red finish and high gloss. Perfect! Closing the shutters and doors to keep the moths and bugs out, she set to work on the base coat. Now that she had the vision for it, excitement danced through her. It'd take a few coats and some strategic sanding to get the finish the way she wanted it, but when it was done, it would look fantastic. Zak would love it.

She painted all night, stopping to wipe sweat from her brow. Rhys was right. Vampires didn't sweat. Only she was sweating now, most likely with a fever like Rhys had said. But why would she have a fever? How could she have a fever? None of it made any sense, so she ignored it. Until it could no longer be ignored. A wave of dizziness swept over her. She straightened, stepping back from the table, can of paint in hand.

"Whoa." The room began to tilt and sway. Her vision blurred. She turned, intending to put her paint can and brush on her workbench. The next thing she knew, she was on the floor, the can of paint rolling away from her, spilling its black contents onto the floor. Her other hand still held the brush, but she couldn't seem to move her fingers to release it. A fire burned in her lungs with each breath. *Shit.* She was in trouble—she really was sick. No matter how much she'd been trying to deny it, the truth was well and truly in her face. Closing her eyes, she focused all her energy on getting her phone out of her back pocket. "Need to call Zak," she muttered. The phone slipped from her fingers. It was there, right in front of her, but she couldn't move. Darkness descended, dragging her into oblivion.

CHAPTER
THREE

Z ak materialized in his bedroom minutes before dawn. He'd had a meeting with his publisher on the other side of the world, a new book deal in the works. It had taken longer than anticipated, and he'd had to cut it short when he received a call from Rhys. He knew it was difficult for the other man to reach out to him, but his worry for Georgia was real. He'd thanked the wolf and wrapped up his meeting as quickly as he could, and came home. He'd fully expected Georgia to be asleep when he returned, but his bed was empty.

Heading downstairs, he found Aston, Dainton, Cole, and Kyan in the kitchen, coffee mugs in hand.

"Hey, Zak," Dainton greeted him, "want a nightcap?"

"Nah, I'm good. Have you seen Georgia?"

"I thought she was in bed. I know Skye went up about an hour ago. She couldn't keep her eyes open."

"No, she's not. Have you seen her at all tonight?"

He could see the cogs turning in their heads as they thought back on the night's activities.

"She went out not long after sunset. She was in her work gear, so I thought she was going to her farm," Cole said.

That made sense. He knew she'd been stressing over finishing his dining table, how it wasn't coming together for her. Maybe she'd gotten caught up in her work and now was stuck at the farm, unable to withstand the sun's rays to get home. That's probably it, he surmised. She'd hunkered down at her farmhouse and was most likely asleep there.

Teleporting to her bedroom at the farmhouse, he was surprised to find her bed empty. And relieved, since her sheer curtains did nothing to keep the sun's rays out of the room. He checked Skye's room, then downstairs. The house was empty. Pushing through the backdoor, he headed down the path to the old barn she'd converted into a workshop. The doors and shutters were closed, but he could hear music playing inside. Pushing open the door, he stepped in, closing the door behind him to shut out the sun, just in case she was inside.

The room was heavy with paint fumes. He eyed the massive table, now painted black. It was streaky in places, indicating she hadn't finished yet. He reached out and touched it. Tacky. He'd left a fingerprint in the paint and grinned...that was going to piss her off. He rounded the end of the table and froze. She was on the ground, out cold. She'd dropped the paint, and it had spilled out of the can onto the floor, looking eerily like a pool of blood.

What alarmed him even more was the slash of sunlight that cut across the floor, peeking through a gap in the shutters, cutting across her forearm that lay exposed. Smoke wafted up from where the rays seared her flesh. The sun had only been up for ten minutes or so, but it was enough to leave an ugly wound. Rushing to her side, he scooped her into his arms, frowning at the warmth radiating from her and the dampness of her clothes against his chest.

Teleporting them to his bedroom, he laid her on the bed. She didn't stir. He removed her clothes, tossing them in the laundry basket. Her skin was damp and clammy, yet sizzling hot. He wet a washcloth in the bathroom and gently bathed her before folding the cloth across her forehead. Still, she didn't stir. He brushed the back of his fingers against her flushed cheeks. If she'd been a hybrid, he might have been able to understand what was happening, but she wasn't. She was a fully-fledged vampire, impervious to infection. How was it possible she had a fever? And why wasn't she healing from the burn the sun had given her? He held her arm. The skin had stopped bubbling and had recovered to a certain degree, but now she had a dark brown scar marring the tender skin between elbow and wrist. What was going on?

He watched over her until sleep became impossible. Giving in to the pull, he climbed into bed next to her, pulling the sheet over them, checking her temperature once again. Still high. He'd have Aston do some research tomorrow.

SHE AWOKE WITH A START, sitting up, clutching the sheet to her chest, breath heaving in great gulps.

"How do you feel?" Zak sat up next to her and placed his cool hand on her forehead. Still hot, but not as bad as yesterday.

"I feel strange," she admitted. "What happened?"

"You fell asleep at your workshop. Got yourself a nasty sunburn." He nodded at her arm. Frowning, she turned her arm over, exposing the burn on the inside of her arm. She ran her thumb across the discolored skin.

"Why is there a mark? Didn't I heal properly?"

"You healed some, but no, not all the way. I'm not sure if the mark will go away entirely. You were sick, Georgia. You had a fever, still have a slight one."

"A fever." It was coming back to her. "That's what Rhys said. I went to the bar, saw him there. He said I was sweating, that I had a fever." She looked down at herself, frowned when she saw the light sheen of perspiration on her skin.

"Zak?" Her voice held a hint of fear.

"We'll find answers. I've never seen this before either. Come on, let's get you cleaned up." He got out of bed and came around to her side, holding out a hand to her. She took it, letting him pull her up. He laced his fingers with hers and led her to the bathroom. It was the first shower they'd taken together that was non-sexual. Carefully, as if she was fragile and might shatter at any moment, he ran his soaped-up hands over her skin, washing away her fever sweat. Then he spun her and washed her hair, fingers massaging her scalp until she groaned.

He wrapped her in a fluffy towel and softly kissed her.

"No matter what happens, I love you."

"I love you too." The shower revived her. She felt stronger already. Maybe the fever was done with her and was on its way out of her system. She shooed him away when he would have helped dress her.

"I'm not an invalid. Go talk with your boys. I'll be down in a minute."

Ten minutes later, she was seated at the breakfast bar, a cup of blood in her hands, her wet hair pulled back into a braid, customary jeans and T-shirt in place. She felt better. More herself.

"Could it have been bad blood?" Kyan asked.

"She would've thrown it up pretty much straight away," Frank answered.

Aston had his laptop out but hadn't found anything useful. The Warriors had all wanted to see the burn. They crowded around her, expressing concern and curiosity. The brown mark hadn't faded, but at least it didn't hurt. Zak had been on his phone when she came down. He'd stepped out to finish the call but returned now to wrap his arms around her.

"Sweetheart, I have to finish up with my

publisher today. I left early yesterday after Rhys called me, but it'll just be a quick trip."

"That's fine, I'm fine. You go. Wait! Rhys called you?"

Zak nodded. "He was worried. Thought you were ill. And knowing you and how stubborn you are, he was concerned you would try and hide it from me."

Georgia pulled a face and looked away. Both men had her pegged. She smiled sheepishly.

"You're looking better. How do you feel?" He was right—she felt better. The headache was gone; she didn't feel the darkness clawing at her insides. He put his palm on her forehead and smiled. "Temperature back to normal. Take it easy tonight. Please!" he added when he saw she was about to argue.

"Okay, fine. I'll take it easy. Whatever it was, I think it's passed now. Now go, sign your deals." She waved him away with a gentle smile. She could see he didn't want to leave her, the doubt swirling in his dark eyes, melting her, wanting her to rush into his arms and never leave. "Go on then," she muttered, looking away, knowing where those looks would ultimately lead. Upstairs to their bedroom, that's what.

"I'll be back soon." And then he was gone. She missed his presence immediately, how her body was so used to having him near that, when he wasn't, it was like she'd moved away from a lovely roaring fire. A shiver ran through her—the warriors caught it, and all looked at her.

"I'm fine. It's one of those 'whose walking over my grave things,'" she assured them, finishing off her breakfast, rinsing the mug, and stacking it in the dishwasher.

"Right. I need to get to the farm. I have a dining table to finish. Whose car can I use? My truck is stuck at the farm."

"I don't think that's wise," Frank said. "Zak wants you to take it easy."

"And I will be. I'm just painting it. It's not exactly hard labor. Regardless, I'm going."

The Warriors looked at each other, hesitating. It wasn't until Skye breezed into the room and told them all to stop being overprotective morons that they relented.

"Fine. Take the jeep. It's out back."

Ah yes, the Jeep that Veronica used to drive. Zak had driven it a time or two when he didn't want to startle the locals with his teleporting powers. The vehicle hadn't been used since Veronica left. Frank opened a kitchen cupboard and removed the keys from a hook on the inside of the door, tossing them to Georgia, who deftly caught them.

Striding out the back door, she crossed to the jeep, where it sat parked alongside the large shed overflowing with building debris. While the house renovations were technically finished, Zak still had a lot of plans for his property, hence the mess in the shed.

Sliding behind the wheel, Georgia slid the keys into the ignition and was about to turn the key when it hit her. The smell. Veronica's scent. It was everywhere. In the leather seats, the seatbelt in Georgia's hand. A switch flipped in her mind. Images of the blonde woman danced before her eyes: the first time she'd seen her in her floral sundress and high heels, at the dance kissing Zak. Her voice filled her head: "Zak's mine. Oh, he might fuck you, but he'll always return to me. He's mine." The words floated in the air, swirling around her. A tiny spark of rage soon became an out-of-control inferno. She slammed out of the jeep, stomped to the shed, and grabbed a piece of wood. Returning to the jeep, she laid into it with the wood, smashing, cursing, crying. Glass flew, windows shattered, light fittings destroyed; not a single panel was spared.

She could hear voices behind her but gave them no heed, her fury overwhelming her until, with a final burst, she lifted the car with her bare hands and tossed it, grim satisfaction in the crunching and groaning of metal as it settled on its roof several feet from where she stood. Breath heaving in her chest, she watched the jeep for a moment, as if half expecting it to right itself. It remained motionless, as did the warriors at her back.

"Georgia," Frank started, but she held a hand out to him, palm out.

"Do not," she breathed, her anger not under control. "I'll be at my farm. I suggest you don't follow." With that, she was gone, sprinting away from them. She ran down the driveway and out onto the road, her vampire speed making her invisible.

The exercise did her good. She arrived at the farm breathless, but her anger was gone, only to be replaced by mortification. *How embarrassing*. She'd gone postal on a defenseless vehicle. What was up with that? Oh, she wasn't stupid; she had a fair idea. Her guilt over Veronica's death still plagued her, and having the woman's presence shoved under her nose like that had triggered her reaction. Looked like becoming a vampire hadn't squashed her hair-trigger temper after all.

Inside her workshop, she surveyed the table, saw the fingerprint, and shook her head in mock irritation. The spilled paint had dried on the cobblestones, and she spent over an hour scraping it off. The brush that had been in her hand when she collapsed was ruined, so she tossed it. Thankfully she had a collection of brushes and rollers, so it wasn't an issue.

After giving the table a light sanding, she was ready to do its second coat. This time she used a roller, and in the paint tray poured half black, half blood-red, letting it mix naturally. Her mind stayed blissfully blank as she worked on the twenty-seater table. In no time at all, that coat was finished. She just needed to let it dry. Cleaning up the roller and paint tray, she stepped outside and walked up the garden path to the swing on her back porch. She settled in, shivering as the autumn air swirled around her legs. She loved this swing. Had loved sitting in it with her morning coffee, catching the early morning sun on her face. It wasn't the same. Although she could see very well in the dark, it was as if the color had been sucked out of her world. Everything was a varying shade of gray.

She felt him before she saw him.

"You're back." She said, not taking her gaze from the washed-out horizon.

"I am." Zak climbed the steps and sat beside her on the swing. "I told you to take it easy."

"I am," she protested. "See, just sitting here on the swing."

"Right after you turned the jeep into scrap metal and *ran* all the way here."

"Sorry about the jeep." She hung her head, ashamed of her behavior.

"I don't give a fuck about the jeep, Georgia. It's you I'm worried about." Reaching out, he placed his hand on her forehead for what felt like the millionth time. "You've still got a slight fever. Not as bad as last night, but it's still there. Are you finished here? For tonight?"

"Yeah. The paint needs to dry."

"You know I can set you up a workshop at my place." He'd offered before, and she'd turned him down. She did again now. "No. I like it here. I created this space for myself. And coming here makes me feel more like me...at your house..." She stopped, unable to look at him.

"What?" He cupped her chin and turned her face to look at him

"I feel like I'm losing myself, Zak." Her voice was

barely a whisper. "I killed a woman. I ripped her heart right out of her chest. Jesus Christ." A single tear tracked down her cheek.

"You were protecting yourself. And your family."

"It still doesn't change what I did. What I have to live with. That can't be me. I don't want that to be me."

"You have regrets?" He'd known it all along. She'd been an innocent human thrown into his evil, violence-filled world. He'd taken for granted that she'd adapted, never realizing how much the blood on her hands would haunt her. He was angry at his own blindness, his inability to see how much she'd been hurting. Hurting and hiding it from him. Is this why she was sick?

"Regret is a wasted emotion," she muttered, pulling back, wiping a hand across her cheek.

"I'm so sorry." He pulled her tightly against him, and she wrapped her arms around his waist, returning the embrace. "Everything has been on my terms, and I've been so selfish. Trying to stop you from coming here, trying to keep you at the homestead all the time. It's just because I want to keep you safe."

"I know." Her voice was muffled against his chest. "But before you? I didn't need to be kept safe. I had room to live." And that was it, wasn't it? He was smothering her, so terrified something was going to happen that would take her away from him that he was pushing her away all on his own.

"Tomorrow, I'm going into town to organize some heavy-duty blackout curtains for this place, and you and I can start spending more time here."

"Sleep here?" she asked, making him wince at the hope in her voice.

"Definitely." His heart hurt a little when she snuggled closer and squeezed a little tighter. Of course, she missed her home. How blind was he that he hadn't noticed? He did notice when her hands started roaming, sliding now around to his chest. Then she was straddling him, setting the swing in motion. He clamped his hands on her hips to help keep her balance and couldn't help but return the sinfully wicked smile on her face.

"I used to have some very hot, very sexy dreams right here on this swing," she purred. Reaching down, she grabbed the hem of her T-shirt and pulled it up over her head.

"Is that so?" His voice was a growl.

"Oh yes. Do you want me to tell you about it?" She reached behind and unclipped her bra, letting it fall to the ground. His fingers dug into her hips, but he kept his hands away from the magnificent vision displayed before him. This was her game; it was his turn to play along.

"Yes." The words were muttered between clenched teeth.

She took one of his hands and slowly glided it in a back-and-forth motion across her belly. "Well, it always started with what seemed like fog, rolling in from the fields. I could feel this presence, this heat, but I couldn't see who it was." Up her hand climbed, dragging his with it. "Only my body knew—how it trembled for his touch, how my heart pounded with anticipation. For this secret dream man? He could do wicked things with his fingers." She placed his hand on her breast, arching into it. He gasped with her at the delicious friction of her nipple in his palm. He played, cupped, and teased, first one breast, then the other. She reached for his other hand and did the same thing, encouraging him with her soft moans.

"And his mouth," she whispered, head thrown back, her beautiful long neck exposed in the moonlight, "the things he could do with his mouth."

Dutifully he leaned forward and placed said mouth against her neck, licking, kissing, nipping until she was squirming in his lap. He lifted her slightly, bringing her breast to his mouth, and sucked her nipple hard. She cried out, clamping her knees against his hips. Oh yes, he knew all her spots.

All finesse gone; he had them both naked in seconds, surging into her as she straddled him, the swing rocking in a crazy rhythm. Clasping her to him, chest to chest, he guided her head to his neck. Tilting his head back, he offered himself to her. She didn't need further prompting. Her fangs sprang out, and she sank them into his neck, pulling deep, drinking his blood. His climax was almost upon him, but he fought it back. This was for her. He'd been way too selfish for way too long, but holding onto his control was difficult; the heat of her fangs in his skin was ambrosia. The more she drank, the harder her hips rocked against him, flesh pounding against flesh. The minute she raised her face from his neck, he bit her, his own fangs sinking into the soft flesh above her breast. Her orgasm tore through her, her body stiffening then tightening around him. With her sweet blood pouring down his throat, he followed her, grunting against her skin.

Wrapped in his arms, sweet aftershocks still rippling through her, Georgia shivered.

"Are you...cold?" Zak's voice sounded puzzled.

"Well yeah, it's freezing out here with no clothes on." She'd begun to shiver, and as he ran his hands up and down her back, he realized her skin did indeed feel cold. He helped her dress, then pulled on his own clothes. Rather than pull on his jacket, he swung it over her shoulders, giving her the extra warmth.

"You do know vampires don't feel the cold. Or the heat." He stood her before him, hands resting on her shoulders.

"And vampires don't get sick either, but I did. And I burnt in the sun...and scarred." But rather than being worried, she seemed happy. And there was nothing more he wanted in this world than for Georgia to be happy. And safe.

CHAPTER
FOUR

T he following evening Zak dragged her outside. He wanted her to train.

"I don't see why you're making me do this. It doesn't work anymore." She pouted, dragging her feet.

"You can teleport, Georgia. I've seen you do it. You've done it once. You can do it again."

"I don't see what the big deal is!"

"Humor me, will you? If I know you can teleport back here, that you can be safe, I can stop worrying about you so damn much."

Maybe he had a point, she conceded. He'd been smothering her because he cared. After all, what she'd endured at the hands of Marius had tortured

Zak too, and he was terrified of something happening to her. She could see he was trying, so she needed to try too. They'd been at it for over an hour with absolutely no progress, not a flicker, and her temper was starting to fray.

"If you're all going to stand around and watch me fail, then you just might find yourself on the end of my blade!" Georgia didn't need to turn around and eyeball the vampire warriors lined up on the back porch to know they were there. She'd heard them arrive even though they'd tried to be stealthy.

"Come on, sweetheart. Focus. You can do this," Zak called to her from across the yard. She eyed the handsome angel-vampire hybrid with jet-black hair, dark as sin eyes, and designer stubble with resignation. He was her friend, lover, mate. And he was right. She could do this. Only right now, she couldn't.

"You can do it." The "it" was the fact that Georgia had teleported from her farm to Zak's house when she was newly turned. When the rogue vampires had turned up looking for a fight to save her sister and best friend Rhys, Georgia had teleported them all. Only that was the one, and only time she'd managed to achieve it. No matter how hard she'd tried since nothing happened. Nada. Zilch. Not even a flicker. She was convinced it had been a one-time thing, a bit of leftover juice in her system from when Zak had turned her—after all, he was the one with the teleporting powers. Zak believed if she kept on practicing, it would happen again.

"I'm done." Spinning on her heel, she headed toward the back steps.

She heard him mutter "Quitter" under his breath, and the next thing, she'd spun and launched herself at him, knocking him onto his back and straddling him as they slid in the dirt. The warriors on the porch sniggered and then groaned when they realized what was coming next. Amidst grumblings of "oh man, they're at it again," they dispersed quickly.

"A quitter, huh?" Georgia perched on Zak's chest, her knees pinning his arms to the ground.

"That's what I said." His lips curled in a devilish grin, his eyes darkening.

Georgia leaned forward and brushed her lips across his. He tried to lift his head to capture her mouth, but she pulled back. *Oh no*. He didn't get to boss her around all day and then be rewarded.

As soon as he felt her relax on top of him, he flipped their positions so she was lying on her back and he was on top of her, only he wasn't sitting on her. He was firmly nestled between her legs. She giggled and wrapped her arms around his neck, pulling his mouth down to hers for a searing kiss.

"Errr, boss. Sorry to interrupt, but we've got company," Frank called from the back door. He was right. The sound of a car could be heard making its way up the long driveway. Zak traced his thumb across her bottom lip, a look of regret sweeping across his face before he moved to his feet, holding out a hand to haul her up.

"Don't recognize the car," Frank told them as they entered the house hand in hand and followed him to the front room.

"Where's Skye?" Georgia asked, looking around for her sister. Even though Skye was a vampire and fast becoming a very skilled warrior, Georgia couldn't shake the deep-seated need to protect and look out for her little sister.

"I'm here." Skye strolled in from the kitchen, a mug cradled in her hand. Her blonde curls were pulled up into a high ponytail, and she was wearing a black pencil skirt, a white-and-black polka-dot blouse, and stilettoes that matched her red lipstick more like her old self. Georgia grinned, a sense of relief rippling through her. Maybe Skye was over the idea of being a warrior?

Georgia didn't miss how Dainton's eyes followed Skye as she sauntered into the room and stood by Georgia's side. The vampire had the hots for her sister. So far, Georgia hadn't been able to work out if Skye returned the warrior's feelings. There was undoubtedly friendship there, and she knew Dainton had helped Skye a lot after her transition.

"Expecting anyone?" Georgia asked no one in particular. Security was pretty tight here. Zak had glamoured most of the townsfolk to take no interest in where he lived, and it was a general rule of thumb that no one visited unless expressly invited.

"Could it be Rhys?" Zak looked down at her, one brow arched. She shook her head. No. The doorbell rang, and Frank opened the door, blocking the view.

"Yes?"

"Oh. Hi." A woman's voice. She cleared her throat. "Umm, I'm looking for Georgia and Skye Pearce. I was told I could find them here?"

Skye clutched Georgia's arm. "Is that?" She turned to her, her green eyes huge.

"Aunt Mel?" the girls said in unison, prying the

door from Frank's grip and throwing it wide open. On the doorstep stood a woman in her late thirties, brown shoulder-length curly hair, hazel eyes, and a smile identical to Georgia's and Skye's.

"Georgia! Skye!" The three women embraced tightly, then Georgia pulled away, eyeing the slightly shorter woman dressed in blue jeans and an emerald green sweater standing before her.

"It's been a while." It came out as an accusation. A look of grief flashed across the other woman's face before she shrugged in apology.

"We've got lots to talk about, girls. I'm sorry I haven't been around much. There's a reason why. Is there somewhere we can talk?"

"Please, come in." Skye grasped her aunt's hand and led her into the house. The Warriors, Frank, and Zak all stood in line, assessing the stranger in their midst.

"Aunt Melissa, these are our friends, Aston, Dainton, Cole, and Kyan. Frank's the guy you met at the door. And this is Zak, Georgia's boyfriend." Skye quickly did the introductions. "Guys, this is our Aunt Melissa. She's my mom's sister."

"I can see the resemblance." Zak stepped forward and dropped a kiss on the back of Melissa's hand. "Welcome to our home."

"Phew, you vampires sure are an overwhelming bunch!" Melissa fanned her face, grinning ruefully at Skye.

"You know about vampires?" Skye asked, brows raised.

"Oh yes. And demons. Wolves. Witches. All the things that go bump in the night."

"How?"

"That's part of why I'm here. Look, sorry, I don't mean to be rude, but this is a conversation I need to have with my nieces. Alone. I'm sure they'll relay it all to you in due course, but...would you mind?"

"I've got a better idea." Georgia piped up. "Let's go to my farmhouse. It'll give us some privacy. If you know about vampires, then you know it doesn't matter where you are in this house; they can still hear you if they choose to stop and listen. Which they will." She flashed them all a look. They had the grace to look guilty. Each and every one of them had intended to eavesdrop on their conversation.

"I'm not sure I'm comfortable with that." Zak crossed his arms over his chest, a stubborn look on his face. Georgia sighed. Crossing to him, she laid a hand on his chest, "I will be perfectly fine. She's not a threat. She's my family. Plus, she'll need a place to stay, so she may as well stay at my place. I'll get her settled in, hear her out, then be home before you know it."

He ran a troubled hand over his face and through his hair. He didn't want to let her out of his sight. She'd been ill, and they still had to work out why. Aston had organized for the ancient books to be taken out of storage in Eden Hills and sent to them; hopefully, there'd be clues in the old texts. But in the meantime, he wanted Georgia by his side.

The memory of their earlier conversation and the realization that she was missing her human life brought him up short. If he didn't give her the space she needed and asked for, he could end up losing her forever.

"Okay." The others looked stunned at his words, but Georgia didn't give him time to change his mind. Snatching up her car keys, she headed out the front door, Skye and Melissa on her heels. "And none of you are to follow us!" she called back over her shoulder. She heard the groans from the warriors, knowing they'd planned to skulk around the outskirts of the farm to "keep them safe."

"YOUR PLACE IS REALLY NICE, Georgia. You did a great job." Melissa stood in the lounge room and slowly spun, taking in the rustic warmth Georgia had projected into the old house.

"Thank you. Please, have a seat. Can I get you anything? Although I have to warn you, I doubt I have anything fresh in the fridge."

"You got coffee? I take it black, no sugar."

"Now that I can do."

Georgia busied herself in the kitchen preparing coffee while Melissa and Skye settled on the couch.

"It's great to see you." Melissa smiled at Skye.

"You too. It's been too long."

"It has. I'm sorry, I should have visited sooner. And more frequently, especially since your mom and dad died."

"Why didn't you?"

"Habit. Jen wanted me to keep my distance from you girls, so it just became a habit that I stayed away. It doesn't mean I don't love you or don't care. I was just trying to keep your mother happy."

"Mom wanted you to stay away from us? But why?"

"Yeah, why?" Georgia placed three cups of coffee on the table and settled herself into the armchair across from the sofa.

"Your mom never wanted you to know this—she'd turned her back on this side of her family—so I want you to know I'm going against her express wishes here, and I don't feel good about it. But you need to know."

"Know what?"

"Our family is descended from a long line of witches—"

"Mom was a witch?" Skye cut in.

"No. No, your mom wasn't a witch. She could have been, but she turned her back on it. Didn't want anything to do with witchcraft, and she didn't want you girls involved either."

"But you're a witch?" Georgia asked.

"Yes. And Grandma was a witch. And Great-Grandma. And so on and so forth."

"How far back?"

"A long, long, long way. We're descended from an ancient witch, Lilura Darkmore. She was a member of the coven of Hester Cromwell, a hybrid witch-angel who created the dagger and ring that bring life and death to immortals."

"You know about the dagger? And Zak's ring?" Georgia frowned. How was this even possible?

Melissa nodded, taking a sip of her coffee.

"But that's not why I'm here." She set her cup down on the coffee table, raising troubled eyes to Georgia, then Skye.

"I'm in trouble," she admitted.

"What sort of trouble?"

"Big, bad, life-ending trouble," Melissa confessed, running a suddenly shaky hand over her face. "There's a witch hunter. Every ten years, he appears and hunts witches. He's relentless. And deadly. After a year of hunting and killing, he disappears. We're not sure where he goes if it's a hibernation thing or what, but every ten years, he awakens, and it's bad news for us witches when he's awake."

"And he's awake now?"

Melissa nodded. "He is. But he shouldn't be because he was awake six years ago. "

"How do you know?"

"That's he's awake? Or that he was awake six years ago?"

"Both."

"Because six years ago, he killed your parents. He's taking out the bloodlines of the original coven. Hester's coven."

"What!"

"But they died in a car accident." Skye frowned in confusion.

"Yes. One he created. He's powerful and devious and has a knack for making his kills look accidental."

"But you never said anything. At the funeral or afterward."

"What good would it have done? You knew nothing of your witchcraft history. I doubt you would have believed me."

"She has a point, Georgia," Skye admitted. "We would have thought she was batshit crazy."

"Why are you telling us now? Because this witch hunter is after you?"

"I believe he is after me, yes, but that's not why I'm telling you. I think he's woken early because the dagger and ring were activated. It was like a power surge of magic traveled the globe when that happened. We all felt it, but only those of us who know the ancient stories knew what it meant."

"You think he's coming for me? Us?" Georgia muttered. "It makes sense. I activated the dagger with my blood. It's my fault Marius rose again. But we killed him."

"But in the process, you killed Zak and brought him back. Along with his memories."

"How did I bring him back? No one can answer that question for me."

"You removed the dagger. If the dagger had remained in his chest, he would remain dead. But only you could remove it; if it had been someone else, he would still be dead."

Silence followed, then Georgia muttered, "I had no idea."

Melissa shrugged. "There's no reason why you would know any of it. Your mother fought so hard to keep you out of magic, but it seems it found you anyway. You were destined."

"Why didn't Mom want us to know? Why did she turn her back on it?"

"Because she was scared. Of the hunter. He killed our parents. He's been slowly taking out our family line."

"He killed Grandma and Grandpa? But they died in a house fire."

"They did," Melissa agreed. "One he orchestrated."

"I don't understand. If Mom was the witch, why kill Dad? Same with Grandma and Grandpa. Assuming Grandma is the witch, why did he kill Grandpa?"

"Convenience. Too hard to get the witch alone. Who knows?"

"Why not kill us as kids?"

"I can't answer that either. Maybe he has a built-in stop switch. I really don't know. All I know is that he's awake when he shouldn't be, and I think he's coming after me."

"So you want us to protect you?"

"No. I want you to destroy him."

"With the dagger?"

Melissa nodded. "And your witchcraft."

"I don't have any witchcraft. And it's too late now. I'm a vampire."

"You've always had the power, Georgia. And you too, Skye. You just need to believe, learn and practice."

"So you're saying I can be a witch and a vampire?"

"Of course."

"THAT'S IMPOSSIBLE. A vampire cannot be a witch." Zak strode back and forth in front of the fireplace, hands behind his back as he pondered what Georgia had told him. Skye perched on the edge of the sofa, eyes following him as he moved back and forth.

"Why not? You're a hybrid, half-angel, half-vampire. It's not inconceivable that I could be a witch and a vampire."

"It's unheard of."

"That doesn't mean it can't be true."

"You want it to be true!" His voice was accusing. Georgia turned from where she'd been gazing absently out the front window, watching the warrior's roughhouse outside as if they weren't listening in on everything that was being said in this room.

"And clearly, you don't. Why not?" She crossed to him, could see the frustration on his face, and was puzzled by it. Would it be so wrong if she were to develop her witchcraft, for she'd realized very quickly that what Melissa had told her was true? It explained her psychic abilities as a human. It made perfect sense.

"It's going to make you a target for this hunter. I just want you safe. After Marius..."

"Sweetheart, I survived Marius. You've taught me how to protect myself. Plus, I have you guys. It'll be fine."

"What about Skye? Are you prepared to risk her

too?" *Oh, low blow.* Georgia glanced at her sister, who was watching them both with interest.

"She's already implicated, Zak. She has magic too. Even if she chooses not to use it, she has it, just like Mom did. Maybe if my mother had learned to use her magic, she'd have had a chance against the hunter."

"Maybe," Zak conceded, blowing out a weary breath. He felt like he'd only just got Georgia back, and someone else was after her. Would she ever be safe? Marius had taken her, fed off her, nearly killed her, yet she'd escaped him. And she'd escaped as a human. Frail. Weak. She'd gotten away and had survived.

His eyes cut to Skye, perched on the edge of the sofa. He'd suggested she should wear a few of the more feminine items from her wardrobe, the type of outfits Georgia was used to seeing her in, and she'd happily obliged. When Georgia had seen her sister in a skirt and heels with makeup on, the relief in her had been palpable. He'd been right. Too much had changed in her world, and she was seriously rattled. He cursed himself again for not noticing, for being totally oblivious to her pain. Now, this. Now magic and witchcraft. He was sorely tempted to lock her away in the cell beneath the house to keep her safe for eternity...a grin twitched at his lips when he imagined how she'd react to that. She'd kick his balls up into his chest cavity for sure. As much as it pained him if he didn't want to drive her away, he had to work with her, not against her.

FIVE

E very day after sunset, Georgia and Skye
traveled to the farmhouse to work with
Melissa for a few hours. Every day Georgia
made progress, and Skye did not.

"Why isn't it working!" Skye stomped her foot
and pouted, arms crossed and looking very much
like a three-year-old about to embark on an epic
tantrum.

"You're blocking," Melissa explained, crossing
the barn where they'd been practicing levitating
small pieces of wood to stand behind Skye and rub
her temples.

"Close your eyes. Take a deep breath in, through
your nose, all the way into your belly, and slowly out
through your mouth. Clear your mind, let your

worries go, let your stress go...concentrate on your breathing."

Georgia watched them from the corner of her eye, trying not to get distracted and drop the three figurines she was twirling around in a circle as if they were dancing. The magic came to her easily. She could feel it inside her, traveling through her veins. It was an intrinsic part of her, a part that she'd had buried deep inside for too long, and now it was running rampant, happy to be free. To be home. From the start, Georgia had taken to magic like a duck to water. But right from the start, Skye had struggled. She couldn't light a candle with a flick of her fingers. Couldn't turn a page in the grimoire by closing her eyes and concentrating. She watched now as Melissa tried to help Skye, but nothing worked. Turning her attention back to her floating figurines, she gently lowered them back to the workbench.

"Is it possible that Skye isn't a witch after all? Maybe it didn't get passed down to her."

Melissa and Skye looked at her, Melissa already shaking her head. "No. It isn't like genetics, where there are percentages involved if you inherit your mother's eyes or your father's. If either parent is a witch, their offspring definitely have magic in their blood. It could be diluted and weak, but it's there. If both parents are witches, then the magic is even stronger and will show up earlier."

"Then why isn't it working for me?" Skye whined. "I'm doing everything Georgia's doing, and not a single thing is working."

"Something is blocking you, Skye. Maybe, secretly, you don't believe any of this, or you don't want any of this."

"But I do. I want super witchy powers like Georgia, to be special like her."

"But subconsciously, maybe you don't. Don't worry, it'll come. We just need to keep working on it. Don't give up."

"Georgia's right. I think I'm not a witch after all. Maybe I was adopted."

"I can prove you're a witch, Skye."

"You can?"

"Yep. Do you want me to?"

"Yes!"

"Okay, cast a circle while I get a couple of things. Warning...I'm going to need your blood."

"Not a problem."

On the workshop floor was a pentagram they'd drawn in chalk earlier; now, Skye went and stood in the circle. Candles were placed at each point of the pentagram, and with her arms outstretched, Skye chanted under her breath. They didn't light. She cast a beseeching look at Georgia, who quickly muttered the same chant, and the candles flared to life, the flames burning brightly before settling into a steady glow.

Melissa joined Skye in the circle, in her hands a metal bowl, a small knife, and a piece of parchment.

"Sit," she instructed. Both women sat cross-legged in the circle, facing each other.

"Give me your hand." Skye held out her hand, palm up. Melissa grasped it and quickly drew the blade across her palm, blood pooling. She tipped her hand sideways, and the blood dripped into the metal bowl. Within seconds the wound had sealed itself.

Melissa chanted softly, a spell the girls hadn't heard before. Steam rose from the bowl, and the blood bubbled. Melissa stopped and opened her eyes.

"Right. If you're a witch, your blood will form a pentagram pattern on this parchment. If you're not a witch, it'll just splatter."

Carefully she tipped the bowl, letting the blood spill out onto the parchment. Immediately the blood began to move, separating and spreading, creating the unmistakable design of a pentagram.

"How do I know you didn't just tell it to do that?" Skye frowned at the parchment. "It doesn't prove that I'm a witch, just that you know some fancy spells."

"Skye!" Georgia admonished, shocked at her sister's accusation.

"You're a witch, Skye," Melissa assured her. Without a word, Skye scrambled to her feet and left the workshop. A minute later, they heard her car start.

"I'm sorry. She's not ready, that's all." Melissa rose to her feet, gathering the bowl, knife, and parchment.

"Why isn't it happening for her?"

"It's true what I said; she's somehow blocking herself. Until that block is removed, she's going to struggle. Now you"—Melissa shrugged—"well, you always had psychic abilities, so you're bound to be more open to the idea of magic and witchcraft. Skye's coming in kinda cold."

"It doesn't have anything to do with my connection to the dagger, does it?"

"Not at all. The dagger is just a weapon. It has

more power when wielded by you, but it is, in fact, just a weapon."

Georgia stood at the workshop door, staring out into the night. There was a chill in the air, summer well and truly over, winter only weeks away. So much had changed.

"Are you still safe here? From the hunter?" Georgia asked. Melissa had been staying at the farmhouse since her arrival in Redmeadows, even though Georgia had invited her to stay at Zak's mansion.

"There's a cloaking spell in place. I'm fine," Melissa reassured her.

"You'll let me know if anything changes?"

"I will." The two women hugged, and as they pulled apart, Melissa pressed her grimoire into Georgia's hands. "Take this. Read it. Practice."

"You're sure?"

"Of course. Now go, help your sister. She needs you."

———

"Going well, I take it?" Zak drawled. Georgia pushed the front door closed with her boot and crossed to him, throwing her arms around his neck and pulling his mouth down to hers. Finally releasing him, she let out a heartfelt sigh. "I needed that." Entwining her fingers with his, she led him into the kitchen, releasing him long enough to rummage in the fridge for a blood bag, talking to him over her shoulder as she emptied it into a mug and placed it in the microwave.

"Skye's blocking, so she's not seeing results, and that's making her mad."

"And you? How's it going?"

"Well!" She grinned at him. "I can do this!" Waving her hands, she levitated the fruit out of the bowl on the counter. She danced them in the air before lowering them carefully back into the bowl.

"Neat." He nodded, but his face didn't seem impressed.

"Just wait until I can do it with bigger items." She wriggled her eyebrows at him, and he laughed.

"What's that?" He nodded at the old leather-bound book she'd placed on the counter.

"It's my family's grimoire. Basically, a book of magic spells the witches in our family have used over the years." The microwave dinged, and she removed the mug, raising it to her lips and taking a long sip. Not as delicious as blood from the vein, but it did the job. "Where's Skye?"

"Sparring with Dainton."

"I should go talk to her. She was really upset." Rinsing the mug, she placed it in the dishwasher.

"I wouldn't. Not tonight anyway. I think she needs some space," Zak warned.

"You reckon? I don't want her to think I don't care that she's struggling with this."

"She won't. She's more like you than you realize. And right now, time out is the answer."

"If you're sure?" Reluctantly Georgia slid the grimoire off the counter and hugged it to her chest. "I was hoping she'd want to read this with me."

"Try her tomorrow."

"Just what did she say to you? Exactly." Georgia frowned suspiciously.

"She was blowing off steam."

"What did she say?"

"Words to the effect that she's had enough of magic and doesn't want to hear the words witch or magic ever again."

"I really should talk to her."

"Tomorrow. Take it from me. You'll make it worse if you force the issue tonight."

"What makes you so sure?"

"Because I deal with you on a daily basis, and like I've already said, you and your sister are a lot more alike than you realize." He softened the words with a wink.

"Okay. I guess." She shrugged, clutching the book tighter to her chest, eager to explore its pages. Zak smiled before quickly kissing her. "Go. Go read your book. I've got some writing to do, then I'll join you." Not needing to be told twice, Georgia skipped from the room, rushing up the stairs to the master bedroom she shared with Zak, bouncing on the magnificent bed she'd made for him and making a nest for herself among the pillows. Balancing the grimoire on her crossed legs, she reverently opened it. The book was old, its pages stiff and yellowed, the penmanship old-fashioned with the occasional blotch of ink. There were diagrams, notes, annotations. It was the door to a new world, and she fell right in.

STRETCHING the kinks out of his neck, Zak switched off his laptop, glancing at his watch. Almost dawn. He hadn't meant to work so late, but he'd just hit send on the email that delivered his latest manuscript to his editor, who'd been hounding him daily. He was behind schedule, with all the excitement of the last couple of months, but thankfully life seemed to be falling back into a familiar rhythm.

Georgia seemed to have shaken off whatever illness had plagued her—he still couldn't get his head around the magic thing, though. Could suppressing magic make you ill? And as much as he wanted to deny that magic could exist within a vampire, Georgia was living proof that it was indeed possible. So far, all she had managed were what he'd term parlor tricks. Not to her face, though. She'd kick his butt into next week if he belittled her achievements.

Thinking of her now, upstairs, waiting for him in their bed, had his lips curling and his body tightening in anticipation. Quickening his steps, he mounted the stairs two at a time.

He stood in the doorway of his bedroom, watching the woman who had him turned inside out sprawled across his bed, asleep. She was a restless sleeper. She'd tossed and turned from the first night they'd spent together, and he'd resorted to simply wrapping her up in his arms and keeping her pinned against him so that they'd both get some rest. Looking at the disarray of his bed now, he knew nothing had changed. The covers were a tangle, and she was face down in the middle, arms spread out to the sides, taking up a lot of space for such a little thing. She'd kicked most of the covers off, the sheet resting just above her backside. He could see the dimples on each side of her spine. She was clearly naked. He was hard instantly.

Approaching the bed, he stripped, leaving his clothes where they fell on the floor. Stopping at the foot of the bed, he crawled up her body; on all fours, he hovered over her, dropping his mouth to those dimples and licking. She was so damn delicious. She murmured in her sleep but didn't wake. Placing a knee on either side of her thighs, he kissed his way up her back, hands skimming along her sides to her shoulders then down her arms, which were still spread-eagled on the bed. He felt her heart rate pick up and smiled against her skin. Her hair was pushed to one side, giving him free rein to the back of her neck, which he took full advantage of, biting and then soothing with slow strokes of his tongue. Her breath hitched, and she pushed her backside into him, hips coming off the bed. Awake.

"Zak..." she whispered, voice heavy with lust.

"I've been thinking about this all evening," he whispered in her ear, making her shiver. "Coming up here to find you in my bed. Naked."

"I want you." She pushed against him again. He knew she wanted to turn over, but he kept her pinned in place. He had all the time in the world, no rush to squeeze in everything he wanted to do to her, with her, for her.

"I'm going to make you scream," he promised, tongue tracing along her shoulder blade.

"Let me touch you," she begged. He loved it when she begged. Begged him to fuck her. Harder. Memories flooded his mind, her taste, the way he fit inside her.

"Not yet," he growled, fisting her hair and pulling her head back to claim her mouth. The move was aggressive, but he took care not to hurt her. Her upper body arched off the bed to meet him, and he took advantage, palming a perfect breast as his tongue explored her mouth. He squeezed and soothed her nipple, and she writhed beneath him. He could smell her arousal, and it nearly undid him. She wanted him as badly as he wanted her.

Tearing away the covers, he pushed her legs apart, settling himself between them and pulling her up onto her knees.

"Grab the headboard." She did, bracing herself. He knelt behind her. Fisting his cock he closed his eyes and pushed into her. He silently apologized for the lack of foreplay; he had to be in her. Now. Her breath sucked in, and they both froze. Oh, God. He could come right now. She was hot, tight, and wet, wrapped around him in dark velvet. She was perfect. Slowly he pulled out, almost all the way, hovering on the edge of her. She tried to push back against him, to take him back in, but he grabbed her hips and held her still. Sweat beaded on his forehead.

"Please. Zak." She panted. He relented, feeling her stretch as he pushed back into her. Then out. *Fuck*. His body was on fire, sweat beading over him. He ran a hand down her back, her skin clammy, covered with a fine sheen of sweat. It felt good that she was just as affected as he. He continued his agonizingly slow pace, and she began to curse him, push back into him even though he tried to hold her in place. She was so responsive.

He leaned over her, stilling, his cock buried deep. His mouth at her ear, he wrapped an arm around her and pressed his thumb against her clit.

"Can you take it rough, baby?"

"Yes!" she all but shouted, body jerking.

He straightened back up and picked up the pace, ramming into her. She met him stroke for stroke, pushing back with each thrust, her skin shining beneath him. Her head dropped forward as she groaned, a long and drawn-out sound that had his balls tightening. Almost. There. The sight of her nape beckoned. Pounding harder, he leaned over her and clamped his teeth into that vulnerable flesh. He tasted blood but couldn't stop himself. He reached under her, his thumb pressing that sensitive spot, hard. She screamed, her climax clenching his shaft so tight. Not releasing her neck, he pounded frantically, finally letting go with a roar, back upright, hands gripping her hips as he emptied into her, flesh slapping against flesh.

She let go of the headboard, her upper body collapsing against the mattress while her ass remained in the air, holding him inside her. Although his legs felt like they were made of rubber, he held his position, not wanting to withdraw, even though his erection was fading. He'd stay like this forever if it meant he could enjoy the view of her submissive pose. Having her submit to him was the biggest turn-on, and what do you know—he was starting to get hard again. She must have felt him twitch because her walls clenched around him, caressing. He got harder. Now that he'd got that first time out of the way, the urgency to reclaim her had lessened. They could go slow, enjoy it more—if that were remotely possible. It didn't matter how he took her, soft and gentle, hard and fast. He loved every second of it.

He traced patterns across her back with his fingertips as he gently rocked into her, keeping the movements shallow.

"Harder," she commanded, her voice muffled by the pillows she had her face buried in.

"Not yet." He was enjoying this too much. He looked down, watching as her wetness glistening on his cock before pushing back into her. Out. In.

"Son of a bitch." She cursed, suddenly using that strength and suppleness that had him awed to lift herself upright, knees between his, now her back pressed flush against his chest, her head resting just below his shoulder. It was harder for him to thrust this way, which was why he suspected she'd moved. She wanted control. She reached up and pulled his head down, her mouth meeting his in a hot, drugging kiss.

Disengaging from him, she quickly swiveled around until she was facing him, legs wrapped around his waist.

"You are fucking amazing." He groaned as she moved up and down while he simply held her. She laughed, then pushed them backward. Now he was flat on his back, and she was riding him, her knees either side of his hips, her face flushed, hair wild around her. Her hips rocked, then swiveled, then she'd let her legs do the work, lifting her straight up, then back down. She reached behind her and massaged his balls.

"I'm. Going. To. Come," he bit out.

"Come for me," she breathed

"Not without you, baby." He was holding on out of sheer will, his body begging for release.

She picked up her pace, riding him hard. His hands gripped her hips as he pumped into her.

"Now!" She cried out, her head thrown back, that glorious mane of hair trailing down her back and tickling his thighs. Her climax pulsed through her, and she grabbed his balls, squeezing. He exploded, grunting as he buried himself in her. *Holy fucking shit.*

"Skye! Come check this out." Georgia was at the breakfast bar, grimoire open in front of her as she sipped her breakfast from a coffee mug.

Skye shuffled over to the fridge, grabbing her own blood bag. "What you got?" she muttered, heating her mug in the microwave.

"It's a daylight protection spell."

"A what now?" Skye slipped onto the stool next to her sister and glanced at the grimoire.

"A spell that allows vampires to walk in the sun. I think."

"Oh wow! Are you going to try it?"

"Of course. I need some stuff for it first, though.

And I should talk to Melissa. She'd warned me not to go willy-nilly with the spells in the book."

"How does it work?"

"Well, I have to get some lapis lazuli, leave it outside in the sun for an hour to harness the sun's energy, then I need to bathe the stone in my blood and say the spell."

"And lapis lazuli is?"

"A gemstone. You've probably seen them around before; they're blue."

"How will you get it outside in the sun? You'll burn."

"Well, Zak is a daywalker. He could do it. Or Melissa."

"Would it just protect you? Or all of us?"

"I think it's whoever's blood you use. So I could do the spell for you if I use your blood. But I want to check with Melissa first. Wouldn't want to mess this one up and accidentally fry you!"

"Who's frying who?" Zak appeared in the doorway, crossing to drop a quick kiss on Georgia's mouth, glancing at the grimoire in front of her.

"Hopefully, no one, but I found this wicked daylight protection spell. Wouldn't it be wonderful if it worked? We could go out in the sun again! I could work in my workshop during the day, and we

might even be able to open the shop again."
Excitedly she turned and clasped Skye's arm.

"Aren't you selling that?" Zak cut in.

"Well, it seems the logical thing to do since we can't operate it ourselves. But with the daylight protection spell, that changes everything."

"We'll have to make a decision soon," Skye said. "The repairs are just about finished."

"What do you want to do with it?" Zak asked.

Skye shrugged. "I'm not really sure. We've been away from it for so long I've kinda lost touch with the feelings it used to evoke. I used to love opening up every day, buying new stuff for Georgia to weave her magic on. I miss it, but at the same time, I don't."

"I agree," Georgia admitted. "I know I miss working on furniture. But the store? I don't know."

They all heard it at the same time. A car pulling up out front. Georgia recognized the rumble of Aunt Melissa's vehicle and rushed to the front door, standing in the doorway watching as her aunt removed the keys from the ignition and slid out of the driver's seat.

"You look like hell." Georgia looked her aunt up and down, taking in the dark shadows beneath Melissa's eyes, her tousled hair, rumpled clothes.

"You say the nicest things." Melissa grinned, shrugging a shoulder.

"No, really. Are you okay? You look beat." Georgia came down the stairs and took her aunt's bag from her. It weighed a ton.

"I am. I've been sourcing supplies and dropping some concealment spells around to throw the hunter off track if he shows up in the area."

"You think he'll find us here?"

"Eventually. I'm buying us some time so we can get you up to speed so you can protect yourself. And Skye."

"And these extra concealment spells will throw him off track?"

"Hopefully." Melissa followed Georgia inside, sliding onto a stool at the breakfast bar, glancing at the grimoire Georgia had been poring over minutes before. "The farmhouse is protected, but considering its somewhat rural location, it'd be relatively easy to find. He'd just scan the area, and that place would show up as a void, so naturally, he'd go investigate, and boom, you're busted. I've scattered a few random concealments on other buildings in and around town, as well as rural places."

"Smart," Zak said, leaning against the sink watching the women.

"It'll only work for so long. But it'll make a good early warning system too. I'll know if he starts poking around. But for now"—she rummaged in the bag Georgia had placed on the counter—"I've got some herbs, gemstones, powders. Enough to keep us going for a while."

"Do you have lapis lazuli?"

Melissa smiled. "I wondered how long it would take before you found that spell. Yes, I have lapis lazuli, enough for everyone."

"So I was right: it is a daylight protection spell for vampires?"

"Correct."

"So the witches have been working with vampires for a long time? This looks old." She indicated the page in the grimoire with its splotched ink.

"When it's beneficial. You'll find that witches, while we like to keep to ourselves, also know when it's wise to align ourselves with other paranormals." Melissa smothered a yawn, apologizing to the group. "Sorry, guys. I'm beat. I've been up for the last twenty hours. I need to grab some shut-eye. Georgia, we'll do your daylight protection spells tomorrow. I'll make sure to set the stones outside tonight, so they'll catch the morning sun. In the meantime, I want you to find, read, memorize the healing spell, protection spell, and the concealment spell."

"READY?" Melissa asked the following evening as they stood in the circle in Georgia's workshop.

"Yes." Georgia's voice wobbled a little. She hadn't realized how nerve-wracking casting her first spell would be. It had seemed simple enough. Melissa had soaked the gemstones in the sun's rays, then stored them in a small black bag with symbols printed on each side and a drawstring tie. Apparently, it held the sun's powers within the stones for a few days. Georgia now had one stone in the palm of her hand and her dagger in the other. It only seemed fitting that her ceremonial knife is the blade she'd found in her workshop months ago, the same one that had brought Zak to her.

"Cut your hand. Drip the blood over the stone," Melissa commanded. Georgia obeyed, sliding the blade across her inner wrist, then holding the wound over the stone nestled in her other palm.

"Say the incantation."

Georgia muttered the words softly, self-conscious. They were hard to pronounce, written in an ancient language she had no knowledge of.

"*Sole slunce tomto kameni, quare me non nechte, quare za denniho ambulabit in lucem.*"

As soon as the words had left her mouth, the blood covering the stone began to sizzle. Her palm burned, but she closed her fingers around the rock and bubbling blood, holding on as instructed. It was working. Well, something was working. Whether she could walk in the sun again, she would have to wait until dawn to find out.

Skye shuffled nervously from foot to foot. Anxiety poured off her in waves. She wiped her palms on the legs of her jeans, watching as Georgia opened her palm to reveal the lapis lazuli stone in her palm, clean and sparkling, with no sign of blood.

"Excellent. Well done." Melissa beamed. "Now, keep your stone in a safe place. It should only be used by you. It's matched to your blood, so you can use it in other spells later on if you need to."

"How long will the sunlight protection spell last? Will I need to keep topping it up?"

"It lasts forever. Or until you cast a spell to cancel it. Just don't use your stone to cast the spell for someone else. It'll taint the blood in the stone and weaken your own protection."

"Gotcha." Georgia tucked the small stone into her front pocket, planning on having it set in a pendant or something so she could keep it near.

"Skye. Your turn."

Skye stepped into the circle and repeated the same steps that Georgia had, only when her blood dripped onto the gemstone in her palm, there was no sizzling, no reaction. Nothing.

"You're still blocking." Melissa sighed. Skye's face fell. They'd hoped she'd manage to beat her subconscious with the importance—and benefits—of the daylight protection spell, but apparently not.

"Come on. I'll do it." Georgia stepped into the circle, and they repeated the process. Georgia didn't touch Skye, just held her hand above Skye's and muttered the incantation. Sure enough, the blood bubbled and sizzled. Skye closed her fingers over the burning stone, wincing, but the pain passed in a second. She opened her fingers again to find the blood gone, her stone shining bright and blue. She smiled weakly at Georgia, her eyes over bright.

"It's okay. You'll get this." Georgia wrapped her in a tight hug, feeling for her sister, who looked so forlorn at not being able to do magic.

They stayed at the farm until dawn. As the sun's rays peeked over the horizon, Georgia tentatively took a step outside. If this didn't work, she and Skye would be spending the day in the workshop with the shutters down. God, she hoped this worked. Zak had texted her several times, asking when she was coming home. She'd promised him soon. He'd threatened to come and drag her home himself, but she promised him she'd be back with a wonderful surprise. He wasn't happy she wasn't under his roof at sunrise but gave her the space she asked.

The sun crested, and a band of light moved surprisingly fast across the ground to where she stood in the pre-dawn light. It hit her toes, then her legs. Nothing. No burning. No smoke. The light traveled up her body until she stood fully bathed in the sun's morning light. She tipped her face up, the warmth on her skin amazing. She'd missed it, hadn't realized just how much until this moment.

"It worked! Come on out," she called over her shoulder to Skye, who remained in the workshop, waiting. Georgia looked back over her shoulder, smiling as Skye and Melissa stepped out, hand in hand. Skye was still nervous, the fear in her eyes fading when she felt the warmth from the sun on her skin. And didn't fry.

"Oh." She gasped, hand going to her throat.

Overcome with excitement, the two sisters squealed and danced, hugging each other tightly.

Melissa smiled at them. "What do you want to do now you are day walkers again?"

"Go into town! Visit the shop. Feel like normal human beings again." Georgia didn't notice the way Skye stiffened at her words.

"Let's go." They piled into Georgia's Ford truck and sped into town. Skye called Zak on the way, giving him the news. He promised to join them in town to help celebrate.

Outside the shop, the girls stood and looked in wonder. It was finished. The doors were locked, but through the big windows, they could see the floor, walls, and ceiling had been repaired. Everything was freshly painted in white. It was a blank canvas ready for them to fill it again. Georgia unlocked the front door, and they stepped inside. The place reeked of paint fumes, so they propped open the front doors for ventilation.

"It's good to be back," Georgia admitted, her voice echoing.

"It is. I wasn't sure I wanted this, but now I'm here? Oh, I can't wait! I can go to auctions again. Get stocked up." Skye's voice rose in excitement, and her eyes sparkled. Georgia hugged her sister. Things were getting back to normal. Well, as normal as they could hope for, being vampires.

"Saw you pull up. The shop looks good." A familiar deep voice sounded from the doorway. Georgia turned to see Rhys standing there, looking as handsome as ever in his police uniform.

"Rhys!" She smiled at him, headed over to give him a hug but halted a couple of feet in front of him, suddenly unsure. She hadn't spoken with him since the night at the pub when he'd called Zak, telling him she was sick.

He looked down at her, his eyes unreadable. Slowly he smiled. Stepping forward, he pulled her flush against his chest in a bear hug.

"I've missed you, troublemaker," he growled softly, releasing her and taking a step back.

"I've missed you too. I'm sorry. About everything." She shrugged. So much had happened, and she'd been through so much without him. For years they'd shared everything. Then she met Zak. Now she was a vampire.

He lifted a shoulder in a shrug. "Shit happens." He strolled further into the shop, looking around. "So the big question is, are you re-opening or selling? The town is abuzz in anticipation."

"Re-opening," the girls said in unison, smiling at each other.

"Oh my gosh, I'm so sorry, how rude. Rhys, this is our Aunt Melissa. Melissa, this is our good friend Rhys."

Melissa stepped forward and shook Rhys's hand. He held onto it for a moment, peering into her green eyes, eyes that were identical to her nieces'.

"You're a wolf," she breathed, assessing him as he was her.

"You're a witch," he countered. She nodded once. He released her hand. She turned to Georgia and Skye. "He's a good man."

"We know."

"Care to tell me how you're able to be out and about during the day?" Rhys was strolling around the empty shop, his back to them. Georgia and Skye looked to their aunt.

"A bit of witchy magic," Aunt Melissa supplied.

"Ah." He nodded, moving back to them, looking down at Georgia with a soft grin on his lips.

"Ladies! The shop's looking good." Zak sauntered in, taking stock of Rhys, Melissa, Georgia, and Skye standing with their arms wrapped around each other. "Congratulations on the daylight protection spell."

"Isn't it amazing?" Georgia launched herself into his arms, and he swung her around, lifting her off her feet. Arms wrapped around his neck, she planted a big, fat, wet kiss on him.

"Congratulations, little witch." He smiled against her mouth.

"Do you believe I can be a witch *and* a vampire now? That it's not one or the other?"

"The proof is before my eyes," he admitted. Across the room, he caught Skye's gaze. She frowned slightly, watching her sister with the handsome angel-vampire hybrid who was her sire. Zak gave her a slight nod, and she relaxed, turning her attention to Rhys and peppering him with questions about what he'd been up to since last she'd seen him.

"You're re-opening?" Zak spoke softly to the woman in his arms. The woman who turned his life inside out and upside down with so little effort and didn't even know it.

"Yes. I missed this. I didn't realize how much until we stepped through that door today, but now that Skye and I can withstand the sun, well, that changes everything."

"Aren't you forgetting something?"

"What?"

"A certain witch hunter who's not only after your aunt but you and Skye as well. You can't exactly be sitting ducks in here."

"Well, naturally, we need to sort out that situation." Georgia pushed away, miffed that he was raining on her happiness. Couldn't he let her enjoy this moment? "We also need to restock. The shop needs a new fit-out. That'll take some time."

"Oh no!" Melissa's hand went to her throat, and she paled, dropping to her knees.

"What's wrong?" Rhys was closest and immediately knelt by her side, his hand on her shoulder. She looked at him with fear in her eyes.

"One of the concealment spells has been broken. He's here."

"Who is?"

"The hunter."

Georgia, Skye, and Zak all looked at each other with concern, while Rhys frowned in confusion.

"Who's the hunter?" he asked.

"A witch hunter, here to take out Melissa, then us. There's no time to explain; we need to get out of here."

"Take your aunt to my house. Cast the daylight protection spell on my warriors so they can join me.

I'll start searching for him now. You three stay at the house."

"Do you know which concealment he broke? That would give them an idea on where to start looking." Georgia asked her aunt.

"East of here. I concealed three houses on Calvern Street." Melissa leaned on Rhys and rose to her feet, pulling herself together.

Without a word, Zak teleported. Did he know Calvern Street? Georgia knew he could only teleport to places he'd visited before...had he toured the whole town in preparation? She knew he'd been busy doing something while she'd been practicing witchcraft with her sister, but whenever she'd pressed him for details, he'd been evasive.

"It's never a dull moment with you." Rhys cussed, striding to the door, knocking the blocks propping them open out of the way so they could be locked again.

"We need to go to the farmhouse first," Melissa insisted. "I need my supplies."

"I'll follow you." Rhys stalked to his car while the women piled into Georgia's truck. Georgia nodded, face grim. She couldn't believe this was happening, just when things started to look up. Booting the truck into life, she quickly reversed, slamming it into first gear and peeling up the street, drawing stares from the townsfolk. Shaking his head in resignation Rhys, jumped into his patrol car and followed, lights flashing and siren blaring. Might as well give the locals something to talk about.

At the farmhouse, Melissa packed her witchcraft supplies in one backpack and her clothes and toiletries in another. Rhys prowled outside, his sensitive nose checking for intruders. Nothing. Skye was on the phone with Frank.

"What do you mean, Zak's in trouble?" she squeaked into the phone. Georgia snatched the phone from her sister's hand.

"What's happened?" she demanded.

"The Hunter has somehow managed to incapacitate Zak," Frank admitted.

"How?"

"No idea. Zak called. Said you were on the way to prep the team, and you'd do your magic mojo on them, then Zak would zap in to collect them and return to deal with this damn hunter."

"So, how do you know something happened to him?"

"Because I heard him scream. Then nothing. I haven't been able to get through to him. You need to get your butt back here now, Georgia, where we can protect you and where you can cast that spell so the warriors can go help him."

Panic flooded through her. Zak couldn't be hurt. He was a vampire-angel hybrid. Indestructible. What had the hunter done? Heart pounding painfully in her chest, she turned with wild eyes to scan the room. Melissa was coming down the stairs, one backpack flung over her shoulder, the other in her hands. She strained under the weight. Skye stood watching Georgia, concern on her face.

"Is Zak okay?" she whispered.

"We don't know. We need to get to the house. Cast the spell for the warriors so they can go help him."

"It's no use. They're just fodder," Melissa muttered, head down.

"What do you mean?" Georgia frowned, snatching the backpack from Melissa's hands and throwing it over her own shoulder.

"Even though they're warriors, they're no match for the hunter. They might slow him down a bit, but they're not going to be able to stop him."

"What *will* stop him?"

Melissa shrugged uncomfortably. "We don't know."

"What?" Georgia's voice rose several octaves.

"I'm sorry!" Melissa cried. "I thought we had more time. I needed to bring you up to speed first, then I was going to take you to the coven. There's a spell we've been working on, but we need more witches."

"How many more witches?"

"Two."

Georgia and Skye. The two sisters looked at each other, then back at Melissa.

"Is this why you came?"

"Partly. And to reconnect with you. It's true what I told you. Your mother didn't want you involved in any of this, but after her death, when the hunter killed her even though she wasn't, nor ever had been a practicing witch, I knew eventually he'd come for you too. We were hoping for more time. He's woken early." Melissa was babbling, her hands fluttering in front of her.

Rhys strode inside, a frown pulling his brows

down. "What the hell is going on?" he demanded. Georgia quickly filled him in, all the while her mind whirling. So, the hunter was a super hunter the witches didn't really know how to defeat, so strong he'd managed to harm Zak with minimum effort and very little time. She suspected Melissa was right, that he'd dispatch the Warriors easily. Zak had been their best defense. Now they were out of options.

"You need to get out of here." Rhys cut through her thoughts.

"I'm not sure we'll be any safer at Zak's house," Georgia said.

"No. I mean out of Redmeadows. You can't hide here. You're as conspicuous as a pimple on an ass."

"We need to get to Azure Falls," Melissa said. "The witches are hiding in the city—the coven always splits when the hunter is awake, but we think that's been our mistake all along. We're stronger united."

"You're also a target."

"It's a risk we have to take. We can't keep running. We need to defeat him."

"Azure Falls is at least three days by car," Skye pointed out.

"I know a quicker way," Rhys volunteered.

"How?"

"My alpha. He owns a small light plane. I might be able to convince him to fly you there. It'll help hide you from the hunter, no passenger manifest."

"Do you think he'll do it?"

Rhys shrugged. "I'll do my best to convince him. He might since it's helping the witches."

Rhys stepped outside to make the call, leaving the three women restlessly waiting. He returned moments later.

"Well?"

"Good news and bad news. Yes, he's prepared to fly you."

"What's the bad news?"

"He can only take two of you. He's taking his mate with him, and it's a four-seater plane."

"Can't he leave her behind and take all three of us?" Georgia asked. Rhys shook his head.

"She's pregnant. There's no way he'll leave her side. She either goes with him, or he doesn't go at all."

Georgia looked at Melissa then Skye. Yes. The two of them would go. She would stay and cast the daylight protection spell on the warriors. She outlined her idea to the others, astonished when Melissa shook her head.

"I need you to come with me, Georgia. We need your magic. Skye's hasn't come in yet. She can't help us while she's still blocking."

"But we need to help the warriors too," Georgia protested.

"If it means you have a better chance of stopping this hunter, then yes, Georgia should go with you," Skye cut in. "I'll stay. I'll do my best for the Warriors. If my magic does come through, I'll know what to do."

"Good girl." Melissa hugged her, pressing a small bag into her hand. "Keep the stones. Keep trying. This just might be the push you need. If your magic comes in, cast a protection spell on yourself, got it?"

Skye accepted the stones, stuffing them into her pocket, nodding.

"No!" Georgia protested. "No. I'm not leaving you. And you said you needed both of us, right? Two witches."

"We do. But Skye can't help without magic. We can only hope that your vampire blood will boost your magic."

"You don't know for sure?"

"You're the first vampire witch."

"Oh my god. Why are you telling me all this stuff

now?" Georgia cried. "It would have been helpful to know that before. Zak was telling the truth: vampires can't be witches."

"It's never happened before. But since it has with you, I'm confident it will work for Skye. You're from the same bloodline, and a powerful bloodline at that."

"Ladies, we need to get moving. We're to meet the alpha at the airstrip. I hate to split you two up"—he nodded at Georgia and Skye—"but you need to make a decision, and we need to get moving. This hunter is smart. He'll probably figure you'll want to get out of town and could be staking out the airport, although he'll most likely be watching the commercial flights, not private."

"Rhys is right. We need to go. Georgia, I'm taking your truck to Zak's. You two go with Rhys to the airport." Skye hurried to the door, determination in every step. Georgia felt Melissa's fingers wrap around hers.

"She's right. We need to move."

Giving in, Georgia allowed herself to be herded outside and bundled into Rhys's car. He sped them to the airport. This time the lights and sirens were off. No need to draw attention to them.

"She'll be okay," Melissa assured her, watching

Georgia's pensive face as she gazed out the car window.

"How do you know?"

"A feeling." Melissa shrugged. "I suspect Zak will teleport her to Azure Falls. You'll be reunited."

"Will her magic kick in?"

"I believe it will."

"Are you just telling me what I want to hear?" Georgia's eyes narrowed.

Melissa laughed. "Not at all. While I can't predict the future, I often get a sense, a feeling."

"And what about yourself? Are you going to survive this?"

"You know we can't sense our own futures, Georgia," she chided. It was true. Georgia had never been able to use her psychic abilities on herself.

They pulled up at a private hangar at the airport.

"It's small." Melissa gulped. "Tiny." On the tarmac stood a two-door white Cessna with a large yellow stripe down the side.

"We'll be okay. Hayden will take good care of us, I'm sure," Georgia reassured her, following Rhys toward the big man and slender woman standing by the plane.

"Hayden, Alison." Georgia nodded at them both in greeting. "Thank you for doing this."

"You're welcome." Alison smiled. "Any excuse to get some baby shopping in. It won't be a wasted trip." Her smile was serene as she rubbed a hand lovingly over the slight bump of her belly.

"Good thing we're dropping you there." Hayden laughed. "We're going to need those two seats to bring back all the shopping this one plans to do." He smiled at his wife, squeezing her into his side as he dropped a kiss on her head.

"We'll stay overnight," Hayden addressed Rhys. "She's going to be tuckered out. I'll give you a call and let you know what hotel we're at. Keep an eye on things while I'm gone."

"You bet." The two men shook hands.

CHAPTER
EIGHT

It was cramped and claustrophobic in the plane. The seats were narrow; Georgia was pressed up against the side of the aircraft on one side and her aunt on the other. Her aunt was already a lovely shade of green and repeatedly clenching her hands on her knees. She was going to have bruises.

With their bags stowed behind their seats, their knees touching the two seats in front, it was a tight fit. Hayden started the engine, and the whole plane vibrated. The noise precluded any chance of conversation, though Hayden and Alison had headsets on and were obviously chatting with each other. By the loving glances they exchanged, Georgia guessed they would enjoy this little getaway. She smiled.

They reminded Georgia of her and Zak, and her smile slipped, replaced by a frown. Was Zak okay? He wasn't dead—she would have felt that through their bond, both blood and mind. Maybe just unconscious, although Frank had said he'd heard him scream. Zak wasn't a screamer. What had the hunter done to him?

The plane shuddered forward, moving to its position on the runway prior to takeoff. Melissa clasped Georgia's hand, crushing it in her grip.

"It's okay. We'll be fine," Georgia told her.

They waited a couple of minutes for clearance. Then they were off, hurtling down the runway, bouncing and jarring, and just when Georgia thought they were going to run out of runway, they took flight, launching into the air. Her stomach flip-flopped then righted itself. She glanced at Melissa, whose eyes were closed, but her mouth moved. Possibly uttering a prayer. Or a protection spell. Her eyes popped open, and she looked at Georgia, grinning sheepishly and slowly releasing her grip on her hand.

Conversation was impossible, leaving them lost in their own thoughts. The higher they got, the colder it grew in the small cabin. Georgia pulled her jacket tighter around herself, glad she'd grabbed it before leaving the farmhouse. That was all she'd had time for, though. Most of her stuff was still at Zak's. She'd have to do some shopping herself in Azure Falls.

Melissa rummaged around in the backpack and pulled out a sweater, pulling it over her head and wrapping her arms around herself for warmth. Not before testing the seatbelt pulled snug over her hips.

They'd been traveling for an hour, slightly more. Melissa was dozing, her head resting against the frosty window. Georgia lost in her own thoughts of Zak and Skye and how they would defeat the hunter when a loud explosion from the cockpit wrenched her from her daydreaming.

Hayden and Alison were screaming in agony; hands bleeding and raw were raised to their faces, steam rising from their skin. Georgia sniffed the air. Wolfsbane. Someone had planted a wolfsbane bomb on the plane. There was a gaping hole in the instrument panel, and the plane was now nose-diving toward the ground, the engine whining.

Georgia tried to reach forward, to grab the controls, but her seatbelt held her back. Releasing the clasp, she wriggled in between the two front seats. Alison was unconscious, her face a red bloody mess, the wolfsbane acting like acid on her skin. Hayden was still conscious, trying to grip the plane's controls with his injured hands.

"I've got it." Georgia pushed his hands away, trying not to hurt him further. "Tell me what to do!" she yelled over the noise of the straining engine.

"Pull it back towards you. Try and get it level—instruments are out, try and get it level to your best judgment." His voice was hoarse, wheezing. Georgia did as he instructed, and the plane leveled out somewhat, although it was still descending at an alarming rate. She looked at him out of the corner of her eye, sucking in a shocked breath. His mouth was almost eaten away from the wolfsbane. She could see him struggling to breathe and knew his airway must have been eaten away as well. How was he still conscious, let alone alive and talking to her?

"Alison," he rasped, reaching his hand in front of Georgia to try and find his wife. Georgia cast another look at the wife and gasped. She hadn't noticed earlier the chunk of metal stuck in the side of her neck, blood seeping down the front of her shirt to pool in her lap. Oh no. Straining her ears over the noise of the plane, she listened for a heartbeat. It was there. Faint. Fading. God, they had to land this plane now and heal them.

"Melissa, can you heal them?" she called back over her shoulder to her aunt, who surprisingly wasn't screaming her head off. No answer.

"Melissa?" She glanced back. Shit. Melissa was slumped back in her seat, her head lolling against the window. Out cold.

Turning her attention back to the controls, she fought to stabilize the plane. She could see the ground below them now that they'd cleared cloud cover. Trees. Lots and lots of trees, and they were heading toward them fast. Too fast. The wheels clipped the treetops, a loud *thwack, thwack, thwack*, then they were lower, tangling with the branches. Trying to keep a hold of the controls that were jerking out of her grip, she drew in a deep breath. They were going to crash.

The plane continued its destructive path through the trees, eventually catching on one and jerking, spinning off in a different direction before hitting another tree and bouncing away again. Time stood still as they barreled through the forest before hitting the earth, sliding through the dirt in a giant plume of dust, sounds of metal tearing, the plane ripping apart. Then suddenly, they were no longer moving. The silence was deafening.

The pain was everywhere. Blinking open her eyes, Georgia quickly closed them again, blinded by the sun blazing down on her. Drawing in a deep breath, then another, she managed to raise an arm and shield her eyes before opening them again. Over to her left was the wreckage of the plane. It had come to a halt with the nose pitched into the dirt, the propeller ripped off, along with the right side wing. The windows on the right-hand side were also missing. Georgia assumed she'd been thrown out since she'd been the only one not wearing a seatbelt at the time of impact. The plane tilted to the left, resting on its one remaining wing.

Gingerly she got to her feet. A sharp nagging pain in her thigh alerted her to the piece of metal poking out through her jeans, blood seeping out, staining the denim and ground where she'd lain. She'd been out for a while, judging by the pool of blood. Gritting her teeth, she yanked the metal free, clamping a hand tightly over the open wound. Ripping off a strip from the bottom of her T-shirt, she tied it around her leg. She'd heal, but in the meantime, she was losing too much blood, and she had to help the others.

Shuffling over to the plane, she wrenched open the passenger-side door. The scent of blood and wolfsbane was heavy in the air, and she closed her eyes. She didn't think Hayden and Alison could have survived the bomb and subsequent crash, but she had to check. Holding her breath, she focused on what she could hear. A heartbeat. Singular. From the back of the plane. Opening her eyes, she forced herself to look at Alison.

"I'm so sorry," Georgia whispered, tears falling down her cheeks. Alison and her baby were dead. She glanced across at Hayden. Dead. Guilt tightened her chest, making her skin crawl. If it wasn't for her, this wouldn't have happened. They'd been here because of her. She'd asked Rhys for help, and this was the result. His alpha and wife were dead, killed, because of her.

A sob tore from her throat as the enormity of it hit her. How was she going to tell Rhys? And his pack? They were going to hate her, blame her for all of this. And they'd be right to. Why had she let them become involved? It was selfish of her.

"I'm so sorry," she whispered, wincing when her eyes landed on the bump of Alison's unborn baby. Her heart ached at the senseless loss of life, at this beautiful little family who had their whole lives ahead of them. Gone, snatched away in an instant by the cruelty of another. Chin lowered to her chest she allowed herself a moment to grieve, then took a deep breath and pulled herself together. The hunter was still coming.

Releasing Alison's seatbelt, she pulled her from the plane and laid her carefully on the ground. She returned to the plane and flipped the seat forward to reach her aunt in the back seat. Her heartbeat was strong and steady, but the bloodstain on her sweater was a worry. Lifting the fabric, she cursed at the deep laceration just above her hip. A gash that was going to need stitches. Or a healing spell, pronto.

"Melissa. Can you hear me?"

"Didn't see this coming." Melissa grimaced, opening her eyes. She sucked in a breath, shuddering.

"Me either. The work of the hunter?"

"Oh yes. He's smart. He always seems to be three steps ahead."

"Will he still come after us? He must think we're dead."

"He'll come. He can sense us. He'll know the crash didn't kill us."

"We'd better get out of here then. I don't intend to be sitting here waiting for him."

Melissa released her seat belt, groaning at the movement. "The others?"

Georgia shook her head. "Let's get you out of this plane, then I can try and heal you." Scrambling back to the door, Georgia jumped down.

"Throw down the bags first, then come to the door. I'll help you down."

Doing as instructed, Melissa tossed down one backpack, then the other, before shuffling to the door, her hand pressed to her side, blood seeping through her fingers.

"Drop. I'll catch you," Georgia ordered. Melissa did so without question, and Georgia realized she was going into shock. She had to heal her, now. Lowering her to the ground, Georgia laid the other woman down, peeling away the edge of her shirt to reveal the jagged torn flesh beneath. Must've been shrapnel from the explosion.

Dragging the backpack that held their spell supplies over to her, she rummaged inside, searching for the herbs she needed. Finding them in a zip lock bag, she dropped a pinch of herbs into her palm and, placing her palms together, she closed her eyes and began the incantation. She hadn't done this before and prayed she was doing it right.

"*Cum moc ve sanabit iniuriae toto emendandum opravit kosti, caro, nervi fetae svaly.*"

The herbs burned and tingled in her palm, and when she opened her eyes, they were gone, her palm glowing. She placed her hand over Melissa's wound and visualized herself healing her, of the flesh knitting together. After a minute, she removed her hand and examined the wound. Not completely healed, but better, much better.

Sitting back on her heels, she blew out a breath. The events of this day had her head spinning. At dawn, she'd walked in the sun, then decided to re-open her shop, had been found by the hunter, Zak had been incapacitated in some way, and now this, a plane crash, miles from anywhere. Did anyone know they were even here? She reached into her back pocket and pulled out her phone. No signal. That figured, given they'd come down in some remote area between Redmeadows and Azure Falls.

Melissa's eyes opened, and she struggled into a sitting position, hand going to the still-bloody wound in her side.

"It's better. I feel better." Melissa's voice was wispy and weak.

"Sorry I couldn't heal you completely."

"You did well. First time too. I'm proud of you."

Melissa blew out a breath and pushed her tangle of curly hair from her eyes. "What now? Hayden? Alison?"

Georgia shook her head. "They didn't make it. I'm pretty sure they died before we hit the ground."

"I'm sorry...was it wolfsbane? I thought I could smell it as I drifted in and out."

"Yeah, it was. How did he know?"

"That we were on the plane? He just does. Obviously, he has some magic of his own."

"Men and their double standards," Georgia groused. She held out a hand and hauled Melissa to her feet.

"Do we bury them?"

"Wolves have their own ceremonies. I don't want to interfere with that. I think they'll be safe enough in the plane from animals. We'll send word to Rhys as soon as we can." Georgia knew it was the right thing to do, but it still felt wrong. How could they just leave them?

Lifting Alison in her arms, she placed her back into the plane, clasping her hand with Hayden's. Tears fell, and anguish tightened her chest.

"Does the radio work? Should we radio for help?" Melissa called. Leaning forward, Georgia grabbed the radio. Nothing. It was dead.

"What do you think we should do?"

"Get away from the wreck. Hike our way out of here and keep heading toward Azure Falls. If we stay here, we're sitting ducks. He planted the bomb on the plane. He probably planted a tracking device too." Georgia bent and grabbed the pack with their supplies and slung it over her shoulders. Melissa followed suit, sliding on her own pack full of clothes.

"Do you know where we are?" she asked.

"No clue," Georgia admitted.

"Well, this is going to be interesting." They both smiled grimly as they headed off into the woods.

CHAPTER
NINE

They stumbled upon the cabin as the sun was setting, just in time. Melissa was losing strength and kept stumbling. Her wound had reopened and was slowly oozing blood. Georgia held her up and dragged her through the cabin door.

The place was rough, unused for many years. But it had windows and a door that closed. It was a one-room shack, a fireplace on one wall, a small kitchen on the other, a bed in the corner, an old sofa in front of the fire. Everything was thick with dust and cobwebs. She eased Melissa down onto the bed, and the woman flopped back, closing her eyes while her chest heaved.

Moving over to the kitchen, Georgia rummaged

through the cupboards. Some tinned food. Out of date by years, but it was all they had. Candles. Half a box of matches. Better than nothing. Setting a candle on the wobbly kitchen table, she lit it, placing another on the mantel over the fire. Rummaging in the cupboards, she found a saucepan, then held her breath as she twisted the kitchen tap. After a lot of groaning, coughing, and sputtering, water eventually trickled out, rusty in color to begin with but soon flowing clear. She filled the saucepan and set it on the kitchen table. No stove, just the empty fireplace. She'd need to gather wood.

"You okay for a few minutes? I'm just getting some firewood."

Melissa waved a hand in the air without looking up. "You go. I'll wait here."

Outside, Georgia foraged for suitable-sized branches to burn in the fire. Her own energy reserves were flagging, and she needed to clean Melissa's wound and have another go at healing her before infection set in and made it even more difficult. The trouble was she hadn't fed in hours, and the scent of the other woman's blood was making her gums ache. While there was food in the cabin that might be okay for Melissa, there were no convenient blood bags for Georgia. It was feed off her aunt or starve.

And her aunt had already lost too much blood; she had none to spare.

Darkness fell, and she began to hear sounds of nightlife, critters moving about among the trees. Looked like she'd have to go hunting. She shuddered at the thought, but animal blood was better than nothing when it came to survival. Carrying an armful of logs back inside, she laid the fire, setting a grate over the top and balancing the saucepan of water over it.

"Melissa?" Her aunt hadn't stirred when she'd returned.

"Hmmm?"

"How are you doing?" She placed a hand against her aunt's forehead. No fever. Good.

"Exhausted."

"I'm going to clean that wound of yours in a little while and do some more healing. But while I'm waiting for the water to boil, I'm just popping out. Okay?"

"Sure." Melissa didn't move, a testimony to her exhaustion.

Outside, Georgia stood and took a deep breath. She didn't know what animals were indigenous to this area. She hoped she could find a decent-sized one so she could feed without killing it. She'd drain a rabbit in two gulps, and just the thought of it made her want to heave. She pulled out her phone and rechecked the signal. Still nothing. And her battery was on twenty percent. Turning it off to preserve what little was left, she tucked it back in her pocket and determinedly walked into the woods.

It wasn't too bad. She'd caught a wild pig, and although it had squealed and wriggled like crazy, she'd managed to feed without killing it. The blood had been bitter, which had helped stop her from taking too much. She'd let the animal go with an apology, wiping its blood from her face as she watched it run into the woods, squealing indignantly.

Back in the cabin, the water had started to boil. Wrapping her shirt around the handle, she lifted the saucepan from the fire and placed it on the sink. She rummaged through Melissa's backpack, pulling out a pale pink tank top. It'd have to do. She dropped the tank top into the hot water and let it soak while she dug through their witchcraft supplies, laying out the bags of herbs on the table, the gemstones, runes, salt, and the grimoire.

Now that she'd fed, she felt stronger—she hoped her magic would be stronger too. Pulling the tank top from the hot water, she squeezed the water out as best she could without giving herself third-degree burns and draped the tank over the back of a kitchen chair to cool for a minute before moving over to Melissa, lifting her shirt and placing the wet cloth against her wound.

Melissa stirred but didn't wake, just muttered in her sleep. With sure strokes, Georgia cleaned away the blood, trying not to let its scent distract her. Satisfied the wound was as clean as she could get it, she dropped the cloth back into the saucepan, the water immediately turning red. Blood soup, maybe? She grimaced, grabbed a pinch of the herbs as before, and clasped them between her palms, chanting as they heated and burned her flesh before leaving her palm glowing. Again she placed her hand directly over Melissa's injury and closed her eyes, this time continuing the chant, forcing more and more of her magic into her aunt.

Pulling her hand away, she examined the wound again. Better, but not fully healed. She cursed, dropping her head for a minute and wishing to God she had more power. But what little she had was better than nothing, she supposed.

Standing, a wave of dizziness assailed her. *Whoa.* Today's magic had really taken it out of her, not to mention being awake for the last twenty-four hours, surviving a plane crash, and only pig's blood to sustain her. She was exhausted and needed rest. Crossing to the sofa, she lay down, the fire bathing her in its glow. The warmth was nice, for the night outside was chilly. With the only blankets in the cabin currently covering her aunt, she didn't relish shivering her way through the night.

Turning on her side, she tucked her hands beneath her cheek and gazed into the flames, watching them leap and lick at the wood. Her thoughts turned to Zak, to the worry that had been niggling her all day. He'd been incapacitated by the hunter. What did that mean? Was he hurt? How badly? The thought of him lying injured brought tears to her eyes. She tried to assure herself that he'd be okay, that Frank and the warriors would find him and heal him. They had to. And what of Skye?

Georgia had vowed she'd never be separated from her sister again. Yet, here she was, miles away, no idea if her sister was safe. However, she felt reasonably confident Skye would be okay since it was Melissa the hunter was stalking. Unless he decided to deal with the lesser threat of Skye in the meantime.

Urgh, she didn't understand any of this. Ancient

witches, vampires, angels. Creating bloodlines that were now wreaking havoc in her once ordinary life. Her exhaustion slowly got the better of her, and her eyes drooped, closing as sleep claimed her.

She stood in the shadowy woods, arms laden with logs for the fire. The wind ruffled through the trees, making them creak and moan. A gust rippled over her skin, and she shivered. Darkness slithered all around her, and anxiety made her shoulders tight. Something was coming for her. The wind growled and echoed around her, and dread weighed heavily as she turned, searching for the threat.

He was coming for her. She had to run.

A deep, menacing laugh echoed around her. She whipped around again, breath caught in her throat. There! In the shadows, the mist surrounding him, the silhouette of a man.

"Who's there?" He moved silently toward her, his feet making no sound. She frowned as he drew closer, heart hammering painfully in her chest, fear holding her in place. She peered into the mist, trying to make out his features. As he neared, she felt it, energy, familiar but different, emanating from him.

"Zak?" She dropped the wood and moved toward him. The closer she got, the more his features were revealed: his dark hair, brooding eyes, strong jaw. Every

time she laid eyes on him, her heart skipped a beat. She still couldn't believe this handsome warrior was hers. Her heart rate picked up, her skin prickled, and a warmth coursed through her. She ran the last few feet and flung herself into his arms. He staggered but regained his balance fast, his hands burning where they rested on her hips, steadying them both. She pressed flush against him, resting her cheek against his chest, his familiar warmth seeping through her, comforting. He'd found her. They were safe.

Something was wrong. His hands remained at her hips, unmoving, while she had her arms wrapped around his waist in a tight embrace. Loosening her grip, she eased back, peering up into his face. He'd been gazing over her head but now glanced down at her. His beautiful brown eyes lacked the heat she was accustomed to. Instead, they were cold, hard. Indifferent.

"Zak?" Confused, she let go, stepping back. "What's wrong?"

Those dark eyes that could melt her with a look flashed. With anger? She couldn't tell. Something within her recoiled, and she backed up another step.

"Do I know you?" He cocked his head to the side, eyeing her up and down, his once cold gaze now hot as he leisurely examined her body. Heat flared between them,

his pull so magnetic it was all she could do not to fling herself back into his arms. His words held her in place.

"What? Are you messing with me?" How could he joke at a time like this?

"Your greeting leads me to believe we know each other." His lip curled in a slow, lazy grin.

"You're telling me you don't know who I am?" Disbelief clouded her voice. How could he not know her?

"You're upset," he deduced with a wry shake of his head. "That's unfortunate. And not my intention." He moved closer. Cautiously, as if he didn't want to startle her, he raised a hand and tucked her hair behind her ear. She frowned at him. That wasn't something he did often. His signature move was to rub his thumb along her lower lip. She could feel her lip tingle now in anticipation. What the hell was going on?

"What is your intention?" she demanded, a flare of anger shooting through her. Why was he jerking her around like this?

"This." Before she could protest, his mouth covered hers. Her anger faded in an instant, replaced by instant lust. Her body heated, melted. A fire burned through her veins. She felt a pulling from deep within, almost as if he were trying to suck out her soul. Again something felt off. She tried to pull away, to break the kiss, but he held firm, both hands coming up to clasp her head in place.

Her desire left in an icy blast. She tried again to pull away, but he held firm and kept pulling the energy from her. Was he stealing her life force? He was doing something—she felt dizzy, weak. She mumbled pleading words into his mouth, but he ignored her. With the last bit of strength she had left, she clutched his jacket and rammed her knee into his groin. That did it. He dropped his hold on her and staggered back, holding his hands to himself and cursing.

Not waiting to see what he would do, she turned and ran.

She woke with a gasp, shooting upright on the sofa, her hand pressed against her racing heart as if to try to stop it from exploding from her chest. What was that? Had Zak dream-walked? Or was she having a nightmare? Rattled, she swung her feet to the floor. The fire had died down, so she tossed another log onto it, holding out her hands to the warmth. She glanced over to the bed where Melissa slept. She hadn't moved an inch since they'd arrived at the cabin yesterday.

The wind howled as it battered the front of the cabin in a sudden gust. The window rattled then stopped. She shivered. Something was off. Something she couldn't put her finger on. She hoped her aunt would be awake and lucid in the morning.

She needed answers, and patience wasn't her strong suit.

Settling back onto the sofa, Georgia couldn't fight the worry that plagued her, making sleep impossible.

TEN

The next day Melissa was well enough to fully heal herself. Still, with the blood loss, they decided they'd wait it out at the cabin for another day so she could rebuild her strength before heading off. Melissa believed a spell would help point them in the right direction to get out of the forest, so she spent the day in front of the fire, flipping through the grimoire.

Georgia couldn't sit still. She walked the perimeter of the cabin over and over, stopping and pushing out her senses. She couldn't shake the feeling from her dream. The feeling that something was coming for them. For her. She knew the hunter was hunting them, it was a given, but even on the plane, when he'd clearly been there and planted the bomb, she'd had no sense of him, had been oblivious to any energy signature he may have left behind. That's what threw her now. Was all of this his doing? This sense of impending doom, the nightmare about Zak—she'd decided it had to be a nightmare. Nothing else fit.

"I'm going to get more wood," Georgia told her aunt, heading for the door once again that evening.

"We have plenty, Georgia," Melissa commented wryly, indicating the stockpile of logs stacked next to the fire.

"I just can't...something feels off."

Melissa looked up from the grimoire she'd had her nose buried in all day. "Everything will be okay. We just need to get to Azure Falls, to my coven."

"I can't help thinking we should have stayed with the plane. Perhaps they would have found us by now."

"The hunter would have, that's for sure. It wasn't safe. We have to go on foot. We'll be fine. I've cast a protection spell. It'll hold us for a while."

"A protection spell? Not a concealment spell?"

"A concealment spell out in the wild? It'll show up as a void and lead the hunter right to us."

Georgia sighed, laying her forehead against the

wooden door. "You're right, of course. I wish Zak were here."

"You're worried about him." It was a statement, not a question.

"Frank said the hunter had incapacitated him. I can't bear the thought of him being hurt. Not knowing what's happening is killing me." Her words came out ragged, her heart yearning for Zak to be held safe in his arms. Especially after the disturbing nightmare.

"He's strong. He'll be fine. The hunter doesn't want him. He wants me. Us."

"Yet he had no qualms about killing Hayden and Alison to get to us."

"It's true he'll do whatever it takes. I'm sorry about your friends. That's why we need to keep moving; it's safer for everyone if we stay away."

Melissa packed up the grimoire and moved to the bed. Settling down, she yawned. "Get some sleep, Georgia. We'll head off in the morning."

Georgia moved to the sofa as her aunt suggested and lay down. She stared again into the dancing flames until her eyes drooped, and sleep claimed her.

"Hello, beautiful." *His deep, husky voice sent vibrations right through her. They were in the woods*

again, and she spun, searching for him. Her eyes zeroed in on a shape leaning against a tree.

"Zak?"

"In the flesh."

She closed her eyes, sucking in a deep breath. When she reopened them, Zak's piercing eyes drew her attention. She couldn't make out his expression, but it was intense. She tore her eyes away, trying to ignore the burning sensation his gaze seared into her skin.

"Is it really you?"

He pushed away from the tree, stalking toward her. She backed up, fear sending an icy trickle down her spine. He looked like Zak. Sounded like Zak. But it wasn't him. The energy was all wrong. Her breath hitched in her throat as she backed into a tree. Suddenly he was there, moving so fast she couldn't track his movements. Raising a hand, he planted it above her head, leaning against the trunk, crowding her. Her body betrayed her, his nearness igniting her senses. Oh yes, her body knew its mate. Sweat beaded on her skin, and she nervously licked her lips. His eyes zeroed in on the movement.

"Who else would it be?" he growled, lips at her ear, his hot breath dancing across her skin, making her shiver. She gulped when his free hand came up and

spanned her throat, his fingers gentle, a soft, slow caress of her skin.

"My best guess is that you're the hunter. In Zak's body." Her voice was barely above a whisper. His fingers stopped stroking and squeezed her neck. She held her breath.

"I guess I blew it by not recognizing you last time we met like this," he admitted, fingers relaxing, easing his grip. She risked a glance into his eyes. They were mesmerizing, the dark depths pulling her in. He was like a drug, her own heroin—this close, all thought was clouded, and all she wanted was her mouth on him, but through the haze, his words penetrated. This wasn't Zak. She jerked her head back, whacking it against the tree trunk with a thump.

"Easy, princess," he murmured, his dark eyes fueling her fire. His voice. His touch. He was undoing her. Remember, Georgia, she scolded herself. It's not him.

"You're not him." She breathed it out loud.

"I knew you were smart. It took me a little while to assimilate his memories, sort through who was who. You pulling me into your dreams took me by surprise. I had no idea he could do that. Or who you were."

"But now you do?"

"Now I do," he agreed. "Georgia Pearce. Once human. Now vampire. And..." He paused, lowering his face to her neck and breathing in her scent. "Oh yes, you are quite the find." He practically groaned the words, his own pleasure thickening his speech. She felt his tongue against the sensitive skin beneath her ear and shivered.

"I can feel his desire for you. It's powerful. Want to know what makes this even more delicious?"

She was breathing in short pants, gasping, trying to hold herself back from the carnal desire rampaging through her trembling body. This isn't Zak, she kept chanting in her mind, but her body didn't believe her. His touch, his smell, his heat—it was all him. She dug her nails into the trunk of the tree, holding herself to its surface to stop herself from reaching for him.

When she didn't respond, he lifted his head, the corner of his mouth tugging up in a smirk at what he saw on her face. "What makes this even more delicious is I can feel your magic, Georgia Pearce. I know what you are. You and your aunt think you can hide from me, think you can run? You're fooling yourselves. But you? Oh, my dear girl." He traced his thumb over her bottom lip, just like Zak used to do. It took every ounce of willpower not to open her lips and suck his thumb into her mouth. "You change everything."

"What...what do you mean?" She gulped, knowing she should be afraid of his words, worried that he knew about her, that she was well and truly busted, but she couldn't break through the lust bubble she was floating in.

"You're my salvation. And the witches doom. You're the key to it all."

"I...I...don't understand..." Talking was so hard, the words thick on her tongue. What was he doing to her? Was he using magic? She felt drugged, heavy, lustful beyond measure.

"All in good time, my sweet Georgia." He cupped her chin, raising her mouth to his.

NO! NO! NO! Her mind screamed. Don't kiss him. It's not Zak. Oh yes, her body quivered, her mouth opening to him, her tongue dueling with his. She reveled in it, groaned into his mouth when he pressed himself against her, his erection hard against her belly, the bark from the tree scraping her back.

Suddenly he froze. Raising his head, he looked behind her, beyond the tree at her back. He cocked his head slightly as if listening, then smiled ruefully, his attention back on her.

"Time for me to go, my little witch."

"What?" Dazed and shaken, all she could do was look at him, this handsome man who turned her world upside down, who was hunting her, not to love her, but to kill her. As he moved back from her, sanity started to return, along with a truckload of regret. Heat burnt her *cheeks at what she'd done with him, what she'd allowed, from a virtual stranger. He chuckled, watching the emotions play across her face.*

"I must go. They've found the plane. The search party starts tomorrow—I'm coming for you." He turned to leave, then quickly swung back as if an afterthought. "Oh, by the way, if you're thinking of telling anyone about this, think again. If you blow my cover with your witchy aunt and her friends, I will order Zak's big, strong, vampire warriors to kill Skye. And they'll do it, for I've already compelled them. And then I'll kill Zak."

"No!" She woke up screaming, drenched in sweat. She rolled from the sofa and onto the floor with a thump. *Oh, God.* Drawing her knees up, she wrapped her arms around them, burying her face, letting the tears flow. Not only did he have Zak, but he also had Skye. She shuddered and rocked, the unforgotten horror of Marius draining her sister, of all they went through. How could this be happening again?

"You okay?" Melissa mumbled from the bed, her voice drowsy with sleep.

"Yes. Sorry, bad dream. Go back to sleep." She wiped her cheeks, drawing a shuddering breath. There'd be no more sleep for her tonight. She considered waking her aunt and insisting they leave now but knew it was pointless. The hunter would catch up with them, she had no doubt, and she couldn't chance incurring his wrath, not while he had control of Zak. And Skye's life dangled in the balance.

ELEVEN

E ven though she thought she wouldn't be able to get back to sleep, exhaustion claimed her, sending her into a deep, dreamless slumber until she was roused by the cabin door flinging open and light pouring across the floor.

"Georgia!" Zak came at her with vampiric speed, pulling her from the sofa and clasping her tightly in his arms. Groggy, she hugged him back.

"Are you all right? Are you hurt?" He ran his hand up and down her back as if reassuring himself she was real.

"I'm fine. We're both okay." She wriggled for some breathing space, and he loosened his hold a fraction, looking over her head at Melissa, who was struggling into a sitting position on the bed.

"There was blood at the crash site. A lot of blood," he muttered, his face dark.

"It wasn't ours. Not all of it. Alison and Hayden, they....they didn't make it." Her voice thickened with tears, but she managed a small smile to reassure him she was okay. The gleam in his eye halted her. *What?* The memory of last night's dream flooded her mind. *It's not Zak!* She stiffened in his arms. He bent his head, his mouth to her ear.

"Easy, sweetheart," he whispered. She nodded stiffly, acknowledging his threat. She had to pretend he was Zak.

"You found them? And the plane?" Melissa stretched and rose from the bed, crossing to the door in the back of the cabin that they'd thought had led outside but instead was a small bathroom that had been added on to the cabin in more recent years.

"The search party did," Zak confirmed. "Once I had your scent, it was easy to follow you here."

Georgia moved out of his embrace and looked toward the open door. "Where's the rest of the search party?"

"Still looking." He shrugged, then winked at her. She bet he'd compelled them to look in a totally different direction. After all, they didn't have the tracking skills he did. When their eyes locked, it was like fire shot through her veins. Her hands ached from wanting to reach out to him, to touch him, but his face was hard. Cold. It made her step back, away from him. Her reaction didn't go unnoticed. His eyes bored into hers, and a whisper of a sardonic smirk crept across his features.

Instead, she crossed to the sink, splashing cold water on her face before leaning her hands against the sink, her head hung low. She felt him behind her but couldn't look at him. Having him here, but not really, hurt. It was different in the dreams. Here in cold hard reality, everything was amplified. Not only her desire for him but her fear and loathing of the man inhabiting his body. Her breath shuddered out of her.

"You're pale." He leaned with his back against the sink, looking at her sideways.

"I'm a vampire." She snickered.

"You know what I mean. You've lost your glow."

"Is it any wonder?" she hissed, straightening and casting him a furious glare.

"She's hungry." Melissa came back in from the bathroom. Grabbing up her backpacks, she tossed them onto the bed to sort through and repack everything.

"Ahhh. I should have realized. You didn't feed?"

"She drank from a pig," Melissa interjected before Georgia could answer. "I'd lost too much blood to be of much help to her."

"A pig?" He chuckled. "You're nothing if not resourceful." He crowded her again, his body too close, his heat enveloping her until she wanted to lean into it and bask in his warmth. Melissa was right, though. She was hungry. Maybe that's why she couldn't hide her reactions around him. She was weak.

"Allow me." Before she could stop him, he'd raised his wrist to his mouth and bitten, tearing into his own flesh. She opened her mouth to protest, but the scent of his blood hit her like a freight train. Her eyes flashed red, and she clamped his wrist to her mouth, guzzling his blood, eyes closed in ecstasy. His blood had always been her favorite.

When she came down from the blood haze, she discovered she was cradled in his arms, her back to his chest, one of his arms supporting her around her waist while she held the other trapped against her mouth. They were on the floor, propped up against a kitchen cupboard. *Oh, my God.* Quickly she released her hold, mortified. She felt the rumble of his chuckle vibrating through her back.

"Better?" His lips brushed her ear, and her head dropped back against his chest of its own accord. The fire of his blood flooding her system had her hyped. Her nerve endings were on fire, and the memory slowly surfaced that she'd only ever fed off Zak in the bedroom because afterward? Afterward, she positively ravished him. His blood amplified her libido tenfold. *Oh dear God*. She closed her eyes, trembling against him, needing a release, hating herself, hating him.

He knew this. He would have seen this in Zak's memories and understood the consequences of drinking his blood. Another shudder wracked her body, and she nearly cried out. She scrambled away from him, scuttling onto all fours, and turned, facing him, her face flushed, her eyes spitting fire. And desire.

"You're magnificent," he breathed, his eyes raking over her. Her body crouched, ready to launch. She trembled, her fingernails digging into the wooden floor, desperately trying to maintain control as the lust, both blood and other, raged through her.

His desire flared. She saw it in the way his eyes darkened and swirled, his scent changed, and her nose twitched as it reached her. No! No, she couldn't let this happen. She was out of the cabin before he could move, running at vampiric speed through the woods.

She fled, pushed faster when she heard him behind her, hunting her, sobbing at the irony. She was running from the hunter. What a pointless exercise. Stopping suddenly, she collapsed to the ground and curled into a ball. Pain, fear, and frustration overwhelmed her, her body shaking with gut-wrenching sobs.

"Ah, little witch, don't fret." He knelt by her side and pulled her to her knees. She didn't fight him, just looked at him with drowning green eyes. He could see why Zak adored her so. She made him want to protect her, and he couldn't have that. She was a means to an end, nothing more. A shutter came down across his features, his eyes turned cold and hard, and he tugged her roughly to her feet.

"Back to the cabin. And you'd better make your aunt believe we made sweet, sweet love out here or—"

"Or what?" Her breath came out on a choked gasp.

"You know what." He eyed her up and down. She was disheveled, with twigs and leaves in her hair, a flush to her cheeks. Oh yes, the aunt would definitely buy that they'd been rolling around fulfilling each other's needs. If it wasn't for the tears.

He reached out and rubbed his thumbs beneath both of her eyes, wiping them away. She tensed at his touch but didn't pull away. Knowing he was pushing his luck, pushing her, he threaded their fingers and led her back to the cabin, daring her to pull away from him. She didn't.

"There you are!" Melissa greeted them at the door. She had the backpacks stacked outside, ready to go.

"Sorry," Georgia mumbled, unable to meet her aunt's eyes, a blush heating her cheeks.

"Perfectly all right." Melissa grinned, shrugging her shoulders.

Georgia cleared her throat, turning to Zak, who still kept a tight grip on her hand. "So, where are we teleporting to?"

"Yeah, about that." He released her hand to run his fingers through his hair. "We're out of luck. My tangle with the hunter damaged my teleporting abilities."

"It did?" Georgia gasped in surprise.

"What happened?" Melissa asked at the same time.

"When I tracked him down, he zapped me with what felt like a lightning bolt. Hurt like the blazes. Knocked me out cold for a while. When I came to, no teleporting ability."

"Do you think it's permanent?" Georgia asked, concerned. He shrugged his shoulders.

"No clue." She watched him, her green eyes darkening. Was he telling the truth? Had Zak really lost the ability, or did the hunter not know how to use them, and this was a cover story? Did it actually matter? Now they couldn't teleport it would mean days trekking through the wilderness until they reached civilization. Unless they made contact with the search party and caught a lift out. Georgia closed her eyes for a moment, undecided on the best course of action. Trekking out of the woods gave her more time, more time to try and come up with a solution to get the hunter out of Zak's body. But if they were rescued, she'd have a better chance of escaping him. Could she risk it? Would he follow through on his threats of killing Skye?

"You're an open book." His eyes flashed, anger sparking as he grabbed her by the wrist and pulled her out of earshot.

"What?" She rubbed her wrist, her own anger rising.

"I can see you plotting and planning, can practically see the cogs turning in that pretty little head of yours. Knock it off."

"Stop telling me what to do. And stop threatening me." Her back was ramrod straight, her eyes spitting fire. He glanced over her shoulder, then brought his eyes back to hers.

"Warned you." Grabbing her by the shoulders, he hauled her up against him and crushed his mouth to hers. She stiffened, then wriggled. His hands slid from her shoulders to wrap around her back, pressing her against him from shoulder to knee. That did it. His heat immediately seeped into her bones, her mouth parted beneath his, and his tongue swept in, capturing her, captivating her, turning her into a puddle at his feet. After an age, he broke the kiss, resting his forehead against hers, both of them panting.

"You've been warned, little witch. Don't blow my cover. If this is the only way I can keep you in line, I'll use it with great delight."

Her breath wheezed in and out of her lungs, and her legs wobbled. She'd only just burnt off the high his blood had given her; having him touch her now was torture. Worse, she knew it affected him too, could feel the rapid beating of his heart beneath her hand, his erection pressing hard against her stomach. Their physical attraction was genuine, and he was right—it was a weapon he could easily use against her. Her eyes filled again, drowning pools of green. He cursed, cupping her face in his hands.

"You need to do better," he muttered.

"It's hard. You're not him." She sniffed.

"Do you want me to be him?" He leered, his insinuation clear.

"I just want him back. Please."

"No can do, little witch. Now. We have an audience. How good an actress are you?"

"You're such an asshole." She cursed, and he laughed. Guiding her back to where Melissa stood waiting, he pulled his phone from his back pocket.

"You have a signal?"

"Nope. But I do have a compass app. We need to head west. This way."

"Where are we anyway? And where are we headed?" Georgia scooped up the heavier of the backpacks and threaded her arms through the straps. Melissa grabbed the other.

"Sullivan National Forest. We're heading to Baxter, which is about fifty miles west. Should take us a day, maybe two." Zak walked around the side of the cabin and retrieved a black backpack he's squirreled away without them noticing.

"Let's go, ladies." He led the way. Melissa fell into step behind him, and Georgia reluctantly brought up the rear. She watched her aunt, worried about the long journey they had ahead of them. There hadn't been much food in the cabin. A can of beans and a can of fruit. She'd consumed them both but hadn't eaten anything today. They'd boiled water to drink but had no bottles to bring it with them. She hoped they'd find water along the way. While she and Zak could manage okay, it was doubtful a human could.

TWELVE

T hey'd been walking several hours when Georgia realized Zak was so far ahead she could barely see him. Melissa's pace had slowed, and Georgia had unconsciously changed her gait to match her aunt's. She looked up as Melissa stumbled, dropping to one knee before struggling to her feet again. She was clearly exhausted.

"Stop!" Georgia placed a hand on Melissa's shoulder, and the woman stopped immediately, turning a tired, sweaty face to Georgia. "You need to rest. Here, sit." She led her over to the base of a tree and helped her down. Melissa let out a long sigh, leaning back against the trunk and closing her eyes.

"I'd kill for a drink right now," she groaned, her voice rough.

"Wait here. I'll catch up with Zak. His GPS map thing might show us where water is. A lake or river or something."

She left her aunt under the tree and ran after Zak. He must have heard her running footsteps, for he'd stopped and was turning back.

"Problem?" He looked as fresh as a daisy as if they hadn't spent the last four hours trudging through the wilderness. He'd removed his jacket and the black T-shirt beneath molded to his muscles. She dragged her eyes away.

"Melissa needs to rest. And water. She needs water."

"Ah yes, delicate humans. I'd forgotten. Here." He swung his backpack around and rummaged around in it, finally pulling out a water bottle and handing it to her.

"You've had this all along?"

He nodded, then handed her an energy bar. "You're welcome," he drawled.

Frustration and anger pulsed through her, but she pushed those feelings down. Fighting with him would get her nowhere. Carrying the water and energy bar back to her aunt, she handed them over before settling at the base of her own tree, sliding her legs out in front of her and tipping her head back to look at the canopy overhead. It really was beautiful, and if she'd been here under different circumstances, she'd have enjoyed it. With a sigh, she cast her eyes to the man who was turning her world upside down.

Zak had settled himself opposite her. She'd felt his eyes on her but refused to look at him until now. His black eyes regarded her coldly, and her breath hitched in her throat. She'd never had Zak look at her with hatred, and it stung. He's not Zak, she reminded herself. But it was his eyes looking at her, eyes that had only ever looked at her with love, lust, and amusement. Never this cold bleakness. The hurt spiraled, curling through her, forming a knot in her stomach. She was unprepared for the shredding of her heart. She jerked her head away, her pain raw, palpable.

He cocked his head, eyes moving to the rock she was absently playing with. As tempting as it was to throw it at him, she dropped it, not missing the grin that swept across his face.

They rested for an hour, and then Zak had them on their feet and moving again. He gave Melissa another water bottle and energy bar and let her lead the way. Their pace was slow going, and Georgia knew they wouldn't reach their destination as quickly as Zak would have liked. He'd consulted his map and changed course slightly, and soon they came across a stream winding through the trees. It was comforting to know they had water. Zak could only fit so many bottles in his backpack.

Georgia wanted to stop and soak her feet in the flowing water, but he pushed them on. She could feel the blisters on her feet, the moisture in her boots telling her the blisters had burst, and she was most likely bleeding. She didn't complain, though. She'd heal. She was more worried about Melissa, whose feet were dragging, dust puffing up as she shuffled along.

"We need to stop for the night." She spoke over her shoulder to Zak, indicating her aunt with a nod of her head. His eyes went past her to the other woman, and he nodded grimly.

"Stop," he called out. Melissa practically sobbed in relief, dropping to her knees, head to her chest.

"Wait here. I'll find a suitable place to set up camp and come back for you."

"Sure."

He moved with lightning speed until he was in front of her, chin held in a hard grip.

"I mean it. Stay here. Don't think of doing anything stupid." His voice was low, his words for her alone. She looked at him, incredulous. Seriously? Her aunt could barely walk. What was she going to do, leave her here with him? Never. He must have read the answer in her eyes, for he let go and was gone.

"Are you okay?" Georgia knelt in front of her aunt, eyes traveling over the sunburnt face, hair drenched with sweat.

"I'm exhausted." Melissa laughed, shaking her head.

"We'll set up camp, and you can heal yourself, right? I don't know about you, but I've got blisters on my blisters!"

"Yeah, pretty sure my feet are a mess. Not to mention my muscles."

Zak returned, eyes traveling over the two exhausted women kneeling in the dirt. He strode forward and swept Melissa up into his arms with a sigh. "Follow me." He directed Georgia. She did. He led them to a small clearing with an outcrop of rocks to one side. While they couldn't see the stream, she could hear it in the distance. She wondered why he hadn't chosen a campsite closer to the water.

"Wild animals," he commented, easing Melissa to the ground. She hobbled over to the rocks and sat on one, untying the laces of her boots and easing them off.

"What?"

"Any wild animals in the vicinity will be attracted to the water. Best to put some distance between them and us."

"Oh. Right." She frowned at him. "How did you know that was what I was thinking?"

"Told you. You're an open book." Disconcerted, she frowned even harder before helping Melissa with her boots and examining the other woman's feet, which were indeed blistered and bleeding. She helped her get what she needed out of the backpack, then stood back and watched while she healed herself. Zak kept a close eye on them but didn't interfere.

"If you want to clean up in the stream, go now, before it gets dark," he told them, gathering wood and dumping it in the middle of the clearing.

Georgia held her aunt's hand, and together they made their way to the stream. Stripping to their underwear, they waded in, the cool water blissful on their sweaty, dusty skin. Melissa splashed around for a minute or two, then started to make her way back to the bank.

"You're leaving already?" Georgia called after her, reluctant to leave the blissful water.

"If I stay, I think I'm going to fall asleep in there and drown. I'm beat. With all the walking and then using my magic, I'm running on empty. I'm hitting the sack."

"Are you okay to get back by yourself?"

"Sure. You stay, enjoy." She waved a hand, not looking back as she hobbled out of sight.

Georgia grabbed the end of her braid and undid the hair tie holding it together. Slipping the tie over her wrist, she shook her hair loose, then dove beneath the crystal clear water, swimming out to the center of the stream where the water was deepest. Pushing to the surface, she floated on her back, watching the sunset paint the sky in stunning streaks of orange, pink, and purple. It was nice to relax, even if only for a moment. All day, her stomach had churned with anxiety over their situation, that and tendrils of anger that kept creeping through. Still, she couldn't afford to lose her cool with "Zak." Her future depended on it.

Speak of the devil, he appeared at the bank. She watched, treading water as he toed off his boots, his intention clear. She should get out of here. Now. His eyes never left hers as he pulled his T-shirt over his head. She gulped, her heart kicking up a notch as the fading light danced across his sculpted chest. Slowly his hands moved to the button on his jeans, flicking it open, lowering the zipper. Still, she stared.

"Really?" he drawled, breaking the trance she'd been in. "I'm all up for it, beautiful." He slid his jeans down his legs, kicking them free. When his thumbs looped into the top of his underwear, he arched a brow as if daring her to look away.

Oh, my God. Clamping her eyes shut, she quickly turned around, breath coming in harsh gasps. She'd forgotten, at that moment, that he wasn't Zak. *Again.* This man who wasn't her man was doing her head in. And now, she was in a potentially explosive situation with him. She hadn't looked away, not until the very last second. She'd let her eyes drink their fill of him, rove over him, memorize each sinew of muscle, the tantalizing vee leading to his groin. *Oh, God.*

She heard the splash as he entered the water. She had to get out of here. Now! Kicking her legs, she swam for the shore, half expecting it when she felt his fingers wrap around her ankle and jerk her to a halt. Her sudden halt had her sinking beneath the surface. He released his hold, and she bobbed to the surface, spitting out water.

"Are you always such a jerk?" she spat, angry at him and even angrier at her reaction to him.

His eyes were black as they regarded her. Before she could guess his intention, he clasped her head between his hands and planted his mouth on hers. Like a spark to a dry forest floor, she went up in a whoosh of flames. His hands left her head to drift across her shoulders, brush past her breasts to rest on her waist, each caress, each touch leaving a path of sizzling flesh in its wake. She groaned into his mouth, her tongue dueling with his.

"My sweet Georgia." He groaned, dragging his mouth from hers to travel down her neck. Her legs wrapped around his waist, and he cursed, his hands digging into her behind and holding her tight. She cried out in bliss when his teeth scraped across her shoulder, bucking against him as he nipped, then soothed with his tongue. She pulled him up; she wanted that mouth on hers. Now. It was hot. He was hot. She couldn't think, only feel, her tongue dancing with his, her hips rocking against him. She felt a tug as her bra gave way, then his palm cupped her breast. Unable to hold back, she arched into him, the movement lifting her upper body out of the water. Taking advantage, he dropped his mouth to her breast, sucking her nipple into his mouth, grazing the sensitive tip with his teeth. She whimpered, blood flowing hot and fast.

"Tell me what you like," he growled against her skin.

It was like a bucket of cold water had been dumped over her head. She stiffened in his arms; then she was pushing, struggling out of his hold, moving back, away. Her slap echoed loudly in the silence. How dare he! How dare he keep using her, using Zak's body.

"Do that again, and you'll regret it," he warned.

"Bite me," she spat. Turning, she waded towards the shore, her long wet hair plastered to her back, hiding her from his view. He grabbed her wrist and jerked her back, but she was ready this time. Her fist swung up, connecting with his jaw and knocking him backward. He lost his footing and fell into the water.

"Don't fucking touch me." Her voice was ice, her body rigid with anger. She stalked away, uncaring that her bra was now floating downstream, and she was wearing nothing but her panties. She scooped up her clothes and clutched them to her chest, hurrying back to camp. Thankfully he didn't follow. She dressed in her jeans and a clean tank top Melissa had left out for her. The sun had set, and darkness obliterated the landscape, bringing with it a chill. She shrugged into her jacket, then pulled her wet hair over her shoulder, squeezing as much water out of it as she could. She settled in front of the fire, staring into the dancing flames and hating herself.

Across from her, Melissa was out, head cradled on her backpack, curled toward the fire, breathing softly and evenly. Georgia envied her. With a sigh and a single tear tracking down her cheek, she pulled her knees up and rested her head on them.

CHAPTER
THIRTEEN

She must have fallen asleep. One minute she'd been in front of the fire, wet hair dripping around her, the next, dawn was streaking the sky, and she was on her side, tucked up against Zak's chest, her hair flowing out in a wave behind her, the warmth from the fire at her back.

"I know you're awake," he murmured, yet he didn't move. Didn't hold her tighter, forcing her to stay. She had no words. Having him so near, waking up in his arms like she always did, only to remember that he wasn't Zak...it was killing her. She hurt in a million different ways and couldn't articulate a single one. Not that he'd care. He was the hunter.

"If it's any consolation," he continued when she didn't respond, "I'm sorry. For last night. It wasn't fair, and it wasn't necessary." His apology was unexpected. Sitting up, she looked at him, her dark hair a wild tangle around her shoulders, the pink streaks tangled within the chocolate strands. Silently he reached up and brushed it away from her face.

"I can't keep doing this," she choked, moving out of reach, even as her body screamed at her to move closer, to lie with him again.

"I know." His face was solemn. He meant it.

More confused than ever, she rose to her feet, brushing the dirt from her clothes and moving to stand by the fire. When she glanced at him over her shoulder, he'd gone. Sighing, she braided her hair and took the empty water bottles down to the stream to refill them. Her aunt was awake and chatting with Zak next to the fire when she returned.

"Zak was telling me we made good time yesterday, that we're still on track to reach Baxter today. Then we can hire a car and drive the rest of the way to Azure Falls."

"That's excellent." She plastered a smile on her face and enthusiasm in her voice. As long as she remembered he wasn't Zak, and he held everyone she loved at risk, she'd get through this.

THAT NIGHT they stayed at a hotel on the outskirts of Baxter. They'd stumbled upon a walking trail late in the afternoon, and following it had led to a parking lot that had led to another hiker packing his gear into his car. Zak had compelled him to give them a lift.

"I'm calling dibs on the shower!" Melissa tossed her backpack on the closest double bed and made a beeline for the door across the room. Georgia wearily stepped inside. Sinking onto the end of the bed, she let out a heartfelt sigh. She heard the shower turn on and couldn't wait for her turn. Covered in dust and sweat, her feet blistered and continually healed. She could feel the dampness of blood in her boots.

Zak closed the door and moved to the second double bed. He'd insisted they all share a room, safer this way against the hunter. She'd almost snorted. Easier for him to keep an eye on her and Melissa more like it.

"Everything okay?" he asked, watching her as she tipped her head back and looked at the ceiling.

"Just peachy, thanks," she snapped.

He laughed. "It'll all be over soon."

"Great. Meaning we'll all be dead. How comforting." *What a douche!* She turned her head to look at him. "And what about Zak? Is he in there with you? Watching all this?"

"No."

"What?" She shot to her feet, alarmed. She'd assumed Zak was a passenger in his own body, that he was still in there somewhere and that when the hunter vacated the premises, he'd be fine.

"Relax. Loverboy isn't dead. But he's not aware. He's not watching all of this and desperately trying to claw his way to you, although that would be a unique and satisfying torture..." He drifted off, probably thinking of ways he could make that happen. "He's sleeping. If I decide to leave his body, he'll awaken with no memories of me and what I've been up to."

"If you decide to leave?" Her voice rose several octaves.

"I quite enjoy his body. It's strong. And the connection between this body and yours? It's tantalizing and addictive. Maybe I won't want to give that up." He shrugged, clearly enjoying her discomfort.

She paced in front of the bed, agitation making

her movements jerky. They both heard the shower shut off, and Zak grinned at her.

"Showtime." He winked. Reaching out, he grabbed her wrist and tugged her down onto the bed. She fell in an awkward tangle on top of him, instantly struggling to get away.

"Keep wriggling, sweetheart." He grinned, one hand wrapping around her nape and the other clasped tightly around her waist. "It's having the desired effect."

"Oh!" She gasped, cheeks flushing. But she stopped struggling.

The bathroom door opened, and steam billowed out. "Hey, can you toss me my bag?" Melissa appeared in the doorway with a towel wrapped around her. Then she noticed them on the bed and grinned. "Oops, never mind. I'll get it." She skipped past them to grab her bag before shutting herself back in the bathroom to get dressed.

As soon as the door closed again, Georgia pushed against Zak's chest. "Let me up, asshole."

"Spoilsport." He released her, laughing again when she shot away from him like a cat on a hot tin roof to stand by the window.

"I'm going to get some food for the human. And I

guess you need to feed too?" He rose to his feet, cocking a brow at her.

She shook her head. Not if it meant feeding on him. The truth was she was starving that she'd barely been able to keep herself from sinking her fangs into the hiker Zak had compelled to drive them. She'd been seated behind him in the car, and her eyes hadn't left the pulse in his neck. Being near her aunt was getting difficult too. The physical demands she'd put on her body today, the constant healing from the sunburn and blisters, had drained her even faster. Unlike Zak, who only needed to feed every few weeks, she was a new vampire and needed blood every day.

"Liar." He moved to the window. Reaching past her, he pulled the curtain aside to peer outside. They were on the ground floor of a budget hotel. She'd been curious as to why he hadn't sprung for somewhere nicer, but this hunter had a plan, and he sure as hell wasn't going to share it with her.

"You do know your fangs are showing, right?" he murmured, letting the curtain drop.

"What?" Her hand flew to her mouth. *Oh shit, he was right*.

"Mmmmm. They're very...sexy." He kept his head close, his voice vibrating through her, making her tingle all over. "They popped out when your aunt opened the bathroom door. Must've been the scent of all her delicious blood pumping through her veins, just waiting for you to take a sip."

"I can't feed on her," Georgia whispered, hand still covering her mouth, her words muffled. "She's not strong enough. She keeps healing herself with her magic, but she doesn't have the inner reserves to spare me her blood."

"Guess it'll have to be me then."

"No." Her voice was a whisper. Pleading. He moved back, watching the storm of emotions cross her face.

"We'll see." He shrugged. The further away he moved, the more relaxed she became. At the door, he tossed her a dark look.

"I'm going to get food for your aunt. Stay here. Don't do anything stupid." The door closed behind him, and she dropped her hand from her mouth with a shaky sigh.

"Shower's free." Melissa plopped down onto the bed she'd claimed as hers and grabbed the TV remote from the night table. "Where's Zak?"

"He's ducked out to get you some food. He'll be back in a minute."

"He's so thoughtful. And I'm starving!" She

switched on the TV and began flicking through the channels. Georgia moved to sit beside her when she felt the weight of her phone in her back pocket. Her phone! Pulling it out, she powered it on. A signal. Not much battery life left, but she had a signal.

"I'm calling home. Back in a sec." She stepped outside, pressing Skye's number. While waiting for the call to connect, she paced back and forth in front of the hotel room.

"Georgia! How are you doing?" Skye's voice crackled through the speaker.

"We're okay. A bit shaken, but we're fine." She moved away from the hotel room, not wanting her aunt to overhear.

"What on earth happened?"

"A bomb. The hunter planted a bomb."

"Who?"

"What do you mean who? The hunter. The guy we're running from? The one who hurt Zak?"

"I don't know what you're talking about," Skye said, her voice skeptical. "Did you hit your head?"

"You don't remember. He's compelled you." She spoke the words aloud as realization hit.

"Zak's not hurt. He's with you, isn't he?" Skye sounded genuinely puzzled.

"Sort of."

"What do you mean?"

"Nothing. It doesn't matter. I just wanted to let you know I was okay."

"Zak already let us know he found you guys."

"He did? When?"

"Couple of days ago."

How could he have? They were in the middle of nowhere with no phone signal.

"What did he say? Exactly?"

Suddenly the phone was wrenched from her hand, flung to the ground, and crunched beneath the sole of a black boot. *Shit.*

"Did I not make myself clear? I said don't do anything stupid." His voice was cold, his eyes angry.

"I was calling my sister. She'd be worried." She crossed her arms over her chest defensively.

"No, she wasn't. I dealt with it. No calling anyone."

"You want me to act normal? This *is* normal! If I've been missing for days, I'd call my family, my friends."

"Who else did you call?" His voice menacing, he backed her up against the side of the building, fingers gripping into her throat.

"No one, dickwad. I had like ten percent battery left on my phone. I only called Skye."

His black eyes flashed steel at the insult, and he hesitated, fingers still tight around her throat before he loosened his grip. Apparently, he believed her.

"You compelled them, didn't you?" she accused, back rigid with anger.

"Get inside." He shoved her toward the door, fury emanating from him. Whirling from him, she did as instructed, storming across the room and into the bathroom, slamming the door behind her. She dimly heard the sound of Zak talking to Melissa as she turned on the taps in the shower. Stripping, she stepped beneath the spray, sighing as the water poured over her, washing away the day's dust and sweat, not to mention the dried blood staining her feet. She stayed under the spray until the water cooled, not caring Zak would be left to have a cold shower. Too friggin bad.

Stepping out, she wrapped a towel around herself, tucking it between her breasts. She grabbed the towel her aunt had used and wrapped that turban-style around her head, then wiped away the condensation from the mirror. She was pale. There were dark shadows under her eyes. And while her fangs had retracted, she could feel them, just beneath her gums, aching. She needed to feed.

Filling the hand basin, she quickly hand-washed

her jeans, T-shirt, and underwear. The water turned a murky brown-red from all the dirt and bloodstains. She looked down at her thigh, where the metal had pierced her when the plane had crashed. While she'd healed, there was now a pale white scar. She frowned, running her fingers over the raised edges. She shouldn't scar. Vampires healed. One hundred percent.

The door opened behind her, and she looked over her shoulder to find Zak leaning against the doorframe, examining her.

"What?" she snapped.

"Just checking." He grinned, his anger from earlier gone. God, his moods switched from Jekyll to Hyde quicker than she could blink.

"That I hadn't crawled out the window? Hardly."

He came inside and shut the door, leaning back against it. She turned her back on him and returned to rinsing out her clothes. Pulling the plug, she squeezed as much moisture as she could out of the clothing before tossing them over the shower rail to dry.

"Shower's all yours." Georgia walked up to him and stared him straight in the eye, refusing to be intimidated. He held her gaze for several minutes before he gave a half shrug and moved away from the door.

Sitting on the side of the bed in the dim room, she unwrapped the towel from her wet hair and shook the strands out, dragging her fingers through them to try and get the tangles out. Melissa had finished the burger Zak had brought and was asleep in the other bed. Glancing at the nightstand, she noticed a hairbrush and helped herself.

As she detangled her hair, she stared at her sleeping aunt. The sound of her heartbeat was loud in the silent room, and Georgia could see the pulse fluttering in her throat. Her fangs descended, and she practically drooled. Hair forgotten, she let the hairbrush drop to the bed and stood, standing between the two beds, eyes intent on her aunt's neck. One tiny sip wouldn't hurt, surely? She was so hungry.

"Are you sure?" Zak's deep voice vibrated against her ear. She didn't acknowledge him but moved slightly closer to her aunt's prone body. He sighed, then his hands landed on her shoulders. She barely registered him, her hunger so great. He pulled her back, but she resisted, her body leaning forward to the blood that was calling her. Just a taste. Her tongue flicked over her fangs.

"I would love nothing more than to let you have at her," Zak continued, one hand tracing lazy circles on the bare flesh of her shoulder and upper arm, "but I fear the ramifications would be more than you could bear, my sweet Georgia."

She glanced at him, irritation pulling her brows together. Her eyes were red, and her lip curled up in a sneer. She was further gone than he realized. Moving in front of her, he pushed her back onto the empty bed and straddled her, pinning her to the mattress. She hissed at him, eyes flashing fire.

"You said it yourself. Your aunt can't spare you her blood right now. If you fed on her, she'd be weak. Very weak. And both you and I need the witches strong."

"We do?" She sounded confused, her eyes unfocused.

"Trust me. We do. So no drinking from your aunt. You can have me instead."

Her gaze focused in on him, her mind processing what he'd said. She loved his blood, she remembered. It did wonderful, wicked, sinful things to her. And then she remembered he wasn't Zak, and she didn't want the wonderful, wicked, sinful things the hunter was prepared to give her.

Tears pooled in her eyes. She was in the ultimate

catch twenty-two. She was so hungry she was prepared to do just about anything. Did that include selling her soul to the hunter? If she had Zak's blood, there would be very little stopping her from taking his body and all that he offered her. The hunter wouldn't stop her; he'd made it perfectly clear he'd be willing to indulge her. And with him on top of her, shirtless, her in only a towel, lying on a bed. Already images were flickering through her mind of them naked, her hips rocking as she rode him, his hands caressing her breasts. Closing her eyes, she shook her head.

"No." Her voice was a whisper, but he heard her. His head tilted. He wiped away her tears.

"You're sure?"

She nodded. He moved off her, surprising her. She'd thought he'd force the issue. She sat up, tugging the towel more securely around her.

"Come here." He stood in the middle of the room, hairbrush in hand. Not thinking what she was doing, she obeyed, standing in front of him, then spinning when he motioned with his finger for her to turn around. She tried to block out the sounds of the heartbeats she could hear from the other side of the thin walls as he worked the knots out of her hair and dragged the brush through, from roots to tips.

Once he was finished, he tossed the brush on the cracked table under the window.

"Get dressed. You still need to feed. I can't have you accidentally tearing your aunt's throat out. We'll just have to go find someone to make a donation."

"Okay." She still stood in the middle of the room. He nudged her toward the bathroom door.

"Starvation makes you much more agreeable, but I think I prefer the feisty version. Go get dressed."

She dropped the towel and walked to the bathroom, not registering the breath he sucked in. Inside the bathroom, she pulled on her wet clothes. They were cold, clammy, and infinitely disgusting. Her face registered her feelings perfectly.

"And maybe we'll get you some new clothes." He grinned as she appeared, most unhappy, in the doorway. "Come on." He held out his hand, and she took it, letting him lead her out of the room. He locked the door after them and pocketed the key.

FOURTEEN

"Pretty sure there's a late-night store around here somewhere." He led them out of the hotel and into the night air with her hand still tucked in his. Out on the street, she realized it wasn't that late. The sun had only just gone down. Funny how exhaustion made her feel like it was already midnight. They walked a fair way, her thoughts not on anything in particular...except blood. God, she was hungry.

"Hah." He grinned, nodding at a shopping center up ahead. The car park was half full, indicating the shops were still open and plenty of people were around. She could feed. And buy new clothes. She was shivering in her damp clothes, her jacket offering her no warmth.

He led her into a large department store and headed straight for the women's section.

"Size?" he asked. She told him, following numbly as he flicked through racks and selected three pairs of jeans, a handful of colorful T-shirts, a hooded sweatshirt, a fleece-lined jacket, a dozen pairs of socks, panties, and two bras. How he knew the size of her bra had her beat. Arms loaded with the haul, she stood and looked at him.

"We're going to need a shopping cart," he surmised, disappearing and reappearing a moment later, pushing a cart. He took the clothes from her and dumped them in.

"Now, let's get you fed. We're going to need a dress."

"A dress?" She was so confused. He nodded and began his search among the racks again, this time coming across a gorgeous floral dress with a sweetheart neckline and long hem.

"Go try this on." He thrust it at her. She looked at him blankly. Why would she need to try it on? He knew her size. It would fit.

With a grin at her tired puzzled face, he wrapped his arm around her shoulder and faced her in the direction of the dressing room.

"Go try it on. Call the girl in to help you. Feed."

"Oh!" Right. Now she got it. Taking the dress from him, she approached the dressing room attendant.

"One item?" the girl asked.

"Yes." Georgia took the colorful tag and proceeded into the dressing rooms. Stepping into an empty booth, she closed the door behind her and shrugged out of her wet clothes. Unzipping the dress, she slipped it over her head and let it settle against her. It was gorgeous. White with a wildflower pattern all over it. The sleeves reached her elbows and were edged in lace, the hem reached just above her ankles, and the skirt flared as she moved. She reached behind her to do up the zipper when she remembered what he'd said. Feed.

"Excuse me, miss?" She stuck her head out the door and called for the attendant. "Would you be able to give me a hand with the zipper?"

"Of course, ma'am." The young girl appeared at the end of the passageway and gave her a friendly smile. Back in her booth Georgia waited. As soon as the girl reached her, she dragged her inside. "Don't scream, don't make a sound, don't move." She wasn't very good at compulsion, hadn't had to use it, but it seemed to work because the girl didn't scream, move or make a sound.

"This isn't going to hurt. Once I'm finished, you won't remember this or me." The girl stood passively while Georgia brought her wrist to her lips and bit down. Blood poured into her mouth, and she swallowed hungrily. She kept an eye on the girl, who simply stood with a blank look on her face. Sooner than she would have liked, she released her grip. More would have been good, but then she'd have a dead body on her hands. She swiped her tongue over the puncture wounds and smiled at the girl.

"Well done. Now zip me up. And can you remove the tag? I don't want to put my wet clothes back on."

The girl did as requested, then left.

Zak was waiting outside the dressing rooms. His face split into a smile when he saw her in the dress. Then he laughed when his eyes landed on her scuffed, dirty boots. She'd left her wet clothes on the dressing room floor; they were ruined anyway. She eyed the cart he was leaning against, pretty sure the contents had grown since she'd been in the dressing room. She dropped the tag from the dress on the top.

"I'll take the dress too." She smiled.

"Feeling better?"

"Much."

At the checkout, she noticed he'd grabbed a sports bag along with a collection of toiletries. He'd thought of everything. He pulled out his wallet and flipped it open, and swiped his credit card. For some reason, it went a long way with her that he'd paid for their purchases and not compelled the sales staff to let them through without paying. Even the dress. The cashier folded all the clothes and packed them neatly into the bag, giving Zak a warm smile when she was done. He thanked her and picked up the bag, ushering Georgia from the store.

Outside he guided her toward a restaurant situated on the corner. She looked at him, puzzled, when he held the door for her. Frowning, she stepped inside.

"What are we doing here?" she whispered as they were shown to a table for two. She sank into the chair the waiter held out for her, absently smiling her thanks.

"I know we don't need to eat, but we *can* eat, and I wanted to do something different with you."

"With me?"

"Just humor me, will you? We don't have to fight each other every step of the way."

"We're not on the same side," she reminded him, crossing her arms over her chest, "You're planning on killing my aunt, my sister, and me."

"It's not personal."

"Pft. It is to me!"

He reached out and grabbed her hand. She frowned at him. What was he playing at?

"I can't help what I am. I was created a hunter. It's what I do. I can't just switch it off."

"Why are you here now? My aunt told me you turn up every ten years, but it's only been six years since you..." *Killed my parents*. The thought ricocheted around in her brain. How could she be sitting in a restaurant with the man who'd killed her parents? His grip tightened on her wrist when she would have stood up, keeping her in her seat.

"I'm sorry." His words were soft, his eyes beseeching.

"Why? Why are you doing this to me?" Her eyes filled with tears, and he sighed, shrugging.

"I'm a weapon. My sole purpose is to destroy the Darkmore witch bloodline. It doesn't matter who gets in my way, how many casualties, as long as I meet my objective."

"But I still don't understand why!"

"It's not my choice." He shook his head, eyes glancing away, then back to her. "I don't have a say in any of it."

"You don't?"

"Nope." He shook his head. Picking up the menu, he began to study it with great intensity.

"Why don't you just...stop then?" She picked up her menu too but didn't look at it.

"I can't. As in I literally, cannot. It's like a force, a power, forcing me on."

"When will it end?" She bit her lip. Probably a stupid question. It would end when the witches were dead.

"I wake every ten years. It's a trade-off for my immortality. I get to live...hunt...for a year, then I sleep for ten. As for when it will end. It won't."

"How long has this been going on?"

"Eight hundred years." He shrugged.

"In the year you're awake, all you do is hunt and kill witches? No fun?"

"Just hunting."

She couldn't imagine his life for the last eight hundred years. No one to care about, no one to care about him. Just wake up, go on an epic killing spree, then back to sleep for ten years. He was existing, not living. He watched, half a smile on his face as she studied him and thought about what he'd said.

"I was created as a weapon, remember? That's all I am. Not a man. A weapon."

"Why are you telling me this?"

He shrugged. "I like you." Her draw dropped. "But..." He held up his hand to silence her. "I have a plan for you. And so do the witches. Don't trust them, Georgia."

"Are you just saying that so they, or I, don't thwart your plans?"

"No."

The waiter appeared, ready to take their order. Zak ordered beer and steak for both of them. Usually, she would have bristled at such chauvinistic behavior, but she let it slide because, well, she actually wanted a beer and steak. This hunter was getting into her head.

When their meal arrived, Georgia was surprised at the wave of hunger that surged over her as soon as the aroma of the meat reached her nose. Her stomach growled, and she placed a hand over it, embarrassed. She hadn't eaten food since becoming a vampire. It hadn't been necessary, and, to be honest, she hadn't given it any thought. Grabbing her cutlery, she dug in, cutting off a strip of meat and popping it in her mouth, chewing with her eyes closed as the flavors burst on her tongue.

"This. Is. Divine." She shoved another piece in her mouth, then cut up the Idaho potato covered in sour cream, shoving that into her mouth too. She glanced at Zak, frowned a little at the big smile on his face, but didn't let that deter her from enjoying her meal.

The food revived her almost as much as the blood had earlier. Sitting back, she took a sip of her beer, the frosty glass cold against her fingers.

"I know you're going to kill me," she began, setting her glass back on the table, "but what about Zak? When you leave his body, will he come back?"

"I can extinguish his soul. Or exit his body with no ill effects."

"And he wouldn't remember any of this?" She waved her hand around the restaurant.

"No. He's not watching through my eyes. He's in a void."

"What about you? Your body, I mean. Where is it?"

"Nice try, little witch." He shook his head, lip curling in a grin.

"Is this how you hunt them? By taking other people's bodies? Because they can't sense you at all when you're occupying someone else?" It was the only thing that made logical sense. Melissa had no clue the hunter had taken up residence within Zak. She was the only one who knew the truth.

He took a drink of beer, eyeing her over the rim

of his glass. Okay, he clearly had no intention of spilling all his tricks and secrets. Fair enough. She still hadn't come up with a plan to get out of this. It wasn't just a matter of physical escape. She had Zak to think about. And Skye. If she got away from the hunter, he could kill them in seconds, with no remorse. She shuddered, looking away.

"Ready to go?"

Nodding, she placed her napkin on the table and rose. As much as she hated to admit it, the evening with him had been enjoyable, and she hadn't planned on that. Enjoying the company of the man who was going to kill you and your family? What the hell was wrong with her?

The walk back to the hotel was in silence. Zak didn't touch her, just walked by her side, matching his stride to hers. Her mind was a whirl of thoughts: how alive her body felt after the meal they'd shared, how she felt so full of energy and power it was as if her feet might float up from the sidewalk and she could take flight. She wanted to talk about it, marvel in it, but she feared the consequences of confiding in him because right now, she felt like she could explode with magic. The very thing he was seeking to extinguish.

"Wait." A thought occurred, and she stopped

dead in her tracks. He stopped and looked at her, dark brow arched.

"Your objective is to kill the witches, destroy the magic, right?" He inclined his head.

"But *you* have magic. To do what you do, you use magic."

"I guess." He continued walking, and she scurried to catch up.

"That doesn't make sense. You're using magic to destroy magic."

"I didn't set the wheels in motion. I'm not the instigator, just the tool."

"But to use magic, you have to be a witch too!" she exclaimed. The change was immediate. His face shut down, anger flashing in his eyes, his shoulders stiff. Dropping the bag containing her new clothes, he grabbed her by the shoulders and propelled her into the trunk of a tree flanking the footpath. Hard.

"Enough!" he shouted, his voice harsh.

"But..."

"NO!" His hand wrapped around her throat, and he lifted her from her feet. Gasping and clawing at his hand, she fought for breath.

"Hey! Everything okay over there?" A car had pulled to a crawl, and a middle-aged man rolled down his window and called out to them. Zak released his grip, and she dropped back to the ground, her own hands massaging her neck.

"Everything is fine," Zak called over his shoulder.

"Miss?" The man didn't believe him.

"I'm fine. Everything is fine," she called out, blowing out a shaky breath.

"You sure? I can give you a lift somewhere," the stranger offered.

"Thank you for your concern, but I'm fine. Thank you." The man eyed her for a little longer before winding up his window and driving off.

"Smart move," Zak muttered, pushing past her to pick up the bag from where he'd dropped it on the sidewalk.

"I couldn't imagine you'd let me leave with him."

"He's lucky he's still breathing as it is. You're pushing the wrong buttons with me, little witch. You'd better be prepared for the consequences. Now move." He gave her shoulder a nudge, and she took the hint, falling into step ahead of him.

STRETCHING, Georgia opened her eyes to sunlight peeking through the curtains. She'd had what felt like the best sleep ever. She'd been pleasantly surprised when digging through the bag of clothes that Zak had bought her pajamas. Admittedly she figured he'd meant them as a joke—Minnie Mouse print cotton pants and a hot pink tank top with Mickey and Minnie kissing in a love heart on the front. She'd laughed when she found them. Hugging them to her chest, she'd hurried into the bathroom to change, snapping the tags off on the way.

He'd been busy on his phone, sitting in the chair by the window. He didn't look up when she returned and slipped into bed unnoticed. She stirred at some point in the night, and his arms had tightened around her, pulling her close, and she fell back into sleep. Now, as she stretched and sat up, he was nowhere to be seen.

"Morning, sleepyhead." Melissa greeted her from the bathroom door. She was dressed, hair brushed, and toothbrush in hand.

"Morning." Georgia flung the covers back. "Where's Zak?"

"Gone to get breakfast and organize a car rental. What's this?" Her aunt indicated the Minnie Mouse pajamas.

"Oh, we went shopping last night after you crashed out. You like?" Georgia laughed.

"With everything I've heard about Zak Goodwin, I would have thought he'd buy you a silk negligee, not cartoon characters." Melissa shrugged. Georgia's smile disappeared. She had a point. Zak would never have bought her something like this...the choice had been pure hunter. It was a sobering thought.

Melissa finished up in the bathroom. "It's all yours."

Throwing her bag onto the bed, she dug out a fresh set of clothes and headed into the bathroom to change. After a quick wash, she slipped into her new jeans, grimacing a little at the stiffness of the denim. She pulled on a purple T-shirt and a gray hoodie. Sitting on the toilet, she pulled on socks and new boots. She eyed herself critically in the mirror as she finger-combed her hair before twisting it into a braid and securing it with the hair tie she kept around her wrist.

Melissa was sitting on her bed, the grimoire in her lap.

"Aunt Melissa?" Georgia sat on her own bed and looked at her aunt.

"Mmhmm?"

"I've been thinking. About the hunter and the witches."

"Yeah?"

"The hunter has to have some magic of his own, right? For him to be able to find you guys, to sleep for ten years, and then awaken? This has been going on for generations, so he's no mere mortal."

"I guess so."

"Is it possible he's a witch? Or at least part witch?"

Melissa cocked her head and scrunched up her face, deep in thought.

"I guess anything is possible," she admitted. "I hadn't really thought about it before."

"So..." Georgia twisted her hands in her lap. "If he's a part witch...is there a spell that could, I don't know, take away his magic? Make him not a witch?"

"Stripping a witch's powers is dark magic. Black magic. It's dangerous."

"But it could be done?"

"Theoretically," Melissa agreed. "But it wouldn't be easy."

"It would be a way to defeat him, though."

"My coven is working on a spell. A spell we've never tried before." Melissa looked back down at the grimoire in her lap and smoothed her hands over it.

"Right, but didn't you say you needed twelve witches? And Skye's not with us to make up the twelve. Plus, her powers haven't come in yet, so basically, you're a witch down. Would the spell still work?"

"That's what I need to talk to my sisters about. I believe you have tremendous magic in you, Georgia. Magic we could amplify for the spell." Melissa lowered her voice and leaned forward. "While I have you to myself for a minute, there's something I must tell you." Georgia automatically mimicked her aunt's movement, leaning in close.

"Witches and vampires? We don't normally mix. There's a natural distrust between the species."

"Right." Georgia nodded. She knew this.

"I don't want to make things awkward for you, but..."

"Oh! I'm a vampire! Will this be a problem for your coven?" Realization dawned.

Melissa smiled. "Not you, dear. You're family, and you're also a witch. It's Zak. He can't be privy to witch business. To our plans. I'm sorry, but I'm going to have to ask you not to repeat any of this."

"No, no, that's perfectly understandable," she assured her aunt, breathing out a sigh of relief. She didn't want Zak, aka the hunter, to know the witches' plans either. Or that she'd been discussing his own magic with her aunt. This was perfect, the perfect cover. She couldn't risk exposing the hunter, not while Zak's and Skye's lives hung in the balance, but neither could she blindly allow the hunter insight into the witches' plans, nor her own plan slowly taking seed. If she could find the spell to strip his powers, he could be defeated. If his powers were stripped, would that bounce him back into his own body? She assumed it would, but she needed time to find the answers first. And she needed the other witches to help her.

FIFTEEN

Azure Falls was beautiful this time of year. The leaves had turned various shades of orange, red and yellow, lining the streets with magnificent color. Zak drove them through the city in the silver Mercedes he'd rented. Georgia had never been in such a luxurious vehicle before and smiled to herself now as she spread her hand across the leather seat beneath her. The car trip had been smooth and uneventful. And quiet. Melissa had been engrossed in her grimoire in the back seat. Zak seemed intent on driving and not conversation, leaving Georgia to continue working on her plan. So far, she had nothing. She blew out a sigh in frustration. She really needed her aunt's grimoire and to bounce some ideas off her, but she couldn't do that with Zak in the vicinity.

"Everything okay?" He glanced at her, eyebrow raised.

"Yeah, sure." Startled out of her daydreaming, she looked at him.

"That was a big sigh."

Georgia shrugged. Zak returned his attention back to driving. Just like in Redmeadows, Azure Falls had a "witches district," an area where they congregated and lived. In Redmeadows, it was along the river; here in Azure Falls, it was just north of the city center. Traffic was heavy, and they spent more time sitting at red lights than actually moving, but eventually they reached their destination, an eclectic, hip inner-city area containing coffee shops, boutique stores, an old movie theater, apartments, markets—a vast range of everything squished into a few streets.

Georgia rolled down her window, feeling the magic in the air. It was stronger than anything she'd ever felt in Redmeadows, its pull on her strong, calling to her own magic, inviting it out to play. She shifted in her seat, fighting the urge to open the car door and bound into the street.

Her aunt placed a hand on her shoulder. "Close the window."

Closing the window, Georgia turned in her seat to look back at her aunt. "Can you feel that? It's powerful."

Melissa smiled at her. "You'll get used to it."

Zak glanced at them both as he inched forward in the traffic. Their hotel loomed ahead of them, so high it cast a dark shadow across the buildings beneath. The Ebony Ribbon Hotel was beautiful; its sleek art deco lines drew the eye to the top, where two towers rose high into the sky. Georgia had seen photos of it before but had never been inside. Five-star hotels weren't her thing, but she had to admit she looked forward to seeing what awaited them. Then immediately felt guilty for such thoughts.

Eventually, they pulled into the curved entrance of the hotel. A bellboy appeared to assist with their bags, and the doorman held the door for them. Before they could walk in, Melissa stopped her with a hand on her arm.

"I'm staying with Tilda at The Black Cauldron, just over there." Melissa pointed vaguely to the streets behind them.

"Oh. You're not staying with us?"

"We have some preparations to do, and I need to

be with my...friends. Here's the address." She pulled a worn business card from her pocket and pressed it into Georgia's hand. "It's a shop, studio, and apartment. Tilda lives there, and I'll be staying with her. We'll need you there tomorrow. Understand?" Georgia nodded, and Melissa hugged her tight, then turned away. Slinging a backpack over her shoulder and carrying the other, she headed off, calling back to Zak, "You take care of her!"

Georgia looked at Zak, who was watching her aunt's retreating back.

"She needs to be with her coven," Georgia said by way of explanation.

"I know." Zak was smiling when he turned back. Wrapping his arm around her shoulders, he led her into the building, where the doorman was still standing patiently holding the door for them.

Their room was out of a magazine. Georgia was convinced she could fit her whole farmhouse in the massive apartment Zak had booked. They were on the top floor; the suite offered two master bedrooms, each with a gigantic bathroom, a large living area with white leather couches, glass coffee tables, and a huge television recessed into the wall. Floor-to-ceiling windows open onto a balcony with a breathtaking view of the city. Everything was elegant and screamed money. Georgia had never felt more out of place in her life.

"Do you like it?" Zak asked, leaning against the doorframe of one of the bedrooms. She turned from where she'd been admiring the view.

"It's beautiful. Luxurious."

He laughed. "And you hate it." Pushing away from the wall, he stalked toward her, his dark eyes swirling. She swallowed, wishing she could back up, but with nowhere to go, she was stuck.

"I didn't say that."

"You didn't have to. It's written all over your face." He stopped in front of her, raised a hand to brush his knuckles across her cheek. "Like you, I have a role to play. Believe it or not, Zak stays in places like this when he travels. Five-star penthouses. I'm surprised he hasn't treated you to a night here."

"Probably because he knows I'd be highly uncomfortable." She defended Zak's decision not to spoil her with such things. She half meant it. She turned her face away from his caress, heard him sigh.

"Tonight will be a night to remember." His voice was cryptic. What did he mean by that? Was he planning something against the witches? She turned suspicious eyes to him, only to find his lip curled in a smirk. "Knew that would get you. Go take a bath. Relax. Luxuriate. I've got a few things to take care of." She sidled past him, stopping when his arm shot out in front of her. "And don't do anything stupid. No phone calls. Don't leave the suite." His words were hot in her ear, and she shivered.

As much as it annoyed her to do what he'd instructed, she did yearn for a nice hot bubble bath. Why not enjoy the amenities while she had them? Their bags hadn't been delivered to the room yet, so she grabbed a fluffy white robe from the bedroom she'd claimed as hers and closed the bathroom door behind her. The bathroom itself was huge, almost the size of her living room. The toilet was discreetly tucked away in the corner, a double-headed shower dominated the middle of the room, and over to the side in its own alcove stood a white bath surrounded by candles. With a wave of her hand and whispered words, the candles flared to life.

Flicking the taps on, she adjusted the water, put in the plug, then dumped in a heavy dose of bubble bath sitting on the edge of the tub. The scent of musk and vanilla wafted to her nose, and she stripped, eager to sink into the scented water. The water poured from the tap like a waterfall, filling the tub quickly. She eased herself into the steaming bath, sighing as it engulfed her. While her muscles weren't aching, the water was definitely soothing. She lay back, not caring that her hair was getting wet. She roused herself long enough to turn off the taps before the bath flooded, then settled back, eyes closed, head resting on the back of the tub.

"I'm almost tempted to join you."

Squealing, she nearly slipped under the water, thrashing to rebalance herself and crossing her arms over her chest. Thankfully she had enough bubbles to hide beneath.

"What the fuck?" she yelled, angry he'd intruded, even angrier that she hadn't heard him approach.

"Sorry. Didn't mean to scare you." His grin told her he wasn't sorry at all.

"What do you want? I thought you went out."

"I've booked us a table at the Ebony Ribbon Restaurant for dinner. Dress up."

"In what?" As much as she didn't want to be hanging out with him, she didn't want to look like a frumpy country bumpkin in a fancy restaurant either. She chewed her lower lip, concern etching her face. Since when did she care about clothes, for god's sake?

"I've organized a dress for you, don't worry. And shoes. Humor me, will you? We need to put on a united front that I'm Zak, and you're the love of his life. Word has got out that we're in town—we need to be seen."

"What if I don't want to?"

"Then you don't value your sister's life as much as I thought you did." He wasn't joking. The cold shutter that came down over his face gave her the chills.

"Fine. Now get out."

He moved before she realized. Leaning over her in the bath, he slid a hand beneath the nape of her neck and lifted her toward him, her upper body leaving the water, bubbles sliding down her breasts and dripping from her nipples. His mouth closed over hers, his tongue sweeping inside before she could protest. Not that she wanted to. At first contact, she melted, her brain conveniently forgetting again that he wasn't Zak. She groaned into his mouth, her tongue meeting his, her heartbeat picking up speed as her stomach tightened and her lady bits tingled.

He pulled back. She opened her dazed eyes to find his gaze on her breasts. She watched him swallow as he slowly lowered her back into the water, the warmth of the water swirling around her sensitive nipples and making them tighten even further. She sucked in a breath and held it. With a wink, he turned and was gone. *What the hell?*

She stayed in the bath until her skin was pruned, playing over the latest kiss with the hunter. Why had he kissed her? To get her to fall in line with his plans? To remind her of the role she had to play in all of this if she wanted to keep her sister safe? Stepping out of the rapidly cooling water, she dried herself off with the most oversized bath towel she'd ever seen, then wrapped herself in the robe. It covered her from neck to toe, and she snuggled into it with delight.

A stunning emerald green dress was laid across the bed in the bedroom, a strappy pair of black sandals placed neatly next to it. Picking the dress up, she admired it as the dress shimmied and caught the light. She wasn't sure what the fabric was, but it was beautiful. It was strapless, a simple sheath that fell from bust to ankle, with a slit along one thigh. And as much as she hated to admit it, she loved it.

And it loved her. Standing in front of the mirror, she swept a hand over her hips, admiring the cut of the dress, how it made her look taller, slimmer. It hugged her curves in all the right places. She'd had to forgo a bra since it was strapless, but the dress had its own built-in paneling that preserved her modesty. The slit in the side allowed her to walk without restriction, and the dress moved and swished around her legs as she walked back and forth in front of the mirror. The black strappy sandals made her ankles and legs look, dare she say it, sexy. Georgia had never thought of herself as sexy, even though Zak had told her countless times. But tonight, in this dress and these shoes, she felt it.

She left her hair down, clipping one side behind her ear with the emerald jeweled hair clip that matched the dress. Using the cosmetics that had arrived with the outfit, she lightly made up her face, giving her eyes a smoky eye effect, a light dust of blush across her cheekbones, and an almost nude lip gloss.

A soft knock at her door shook her out of admiring her own reflection. She had a slight grin turning up the corners of her lips when she opened the bedroom door to find Zak standing on the other side dressed in a black suit and crisp white shirt with a matching black tie. She sucked in a breath. *Holy shit*. She'd never seen him dressed this way before. He was stunning. And sexy as hell.

"You look beautiful." His words were soft, his face sincere.

"Thank you. So do you." He smirked, and she rushed on. "Not beautiful, that is. Handsome. You look handsome. Oh my God! Why am I saying that to you?" Nerves were getting the better of her, her hands gesturing wildly.

"Relax. Take a breath." Wrapping his hand around her upper arm, he led her out into the living area, stopping just before they left the suite. "Ready? Remember, tonight has to be believable."

"Got it," she croaked. She had a feeling it would be all too believable because right now, her libido was doing funny things to her stomach. She didn't want to leave the suite. She wanted to toss him to the floor and ravish him, Zak or not. And those were very dangerous, alarming thoughts.

He led her to the elevator, his hand burning where it rested on her lower back. He matched his pace to hers, slowing as she got used to walking in the heels without falling flat on her face. The elevator ride was short. She'd kept her eyes closed the whole way because on each wall was a full-length mirror, reflecting images of her and Zak, so perfectly suited, burning into her retinas. Her hands clenched into fists to keep herself from clutching his lapels and dragging his mouth to hers.

"You're doing great." His wolfish smile told her he knew what she was feeling. Taking her hand, he led her out into the restaurant's foyer. Cameras flashed in her face, making her blink.

"What the hell?" she muttered, trying to clear the spots from her eyes.

"Paparazzi," Zak whispered in her ear. "Smile and pretend you like me, or even better, remember that kiss in the bath, the way your tongue stroked mine, the way the water ran off your breasts, how you burned for my touch."

A flush darkened her cheeks as his words painted an all too real picture in her mind. She looked up at him, her eyes flashing.

"That's it, sweetheart," he murmured, his lip twisting in a half-smile. "You are so fucking stunning. It's all I can do not to push you back into that elevator and fuck you senseless." He wrapped a hand around her neck and pressed his mouth to hers. She was dimly aware of cameras clicking and flashing around them, but she was lost. Lost in his touch, his taste, the words he'd told her. She whimpered when he pulled away.

"Well done." He dropped a quick kiss on her

cheek and then straightened. With his arm around her waist, he guided her into the restaurant. She feared if he took his arm away, she'd collapse at his feet, for her legs felt as useless as wet noodles.

They were seated at an intimate table for two, shielded from view by towering palms. Georgia blew out a breath and tried to get her bearings. Thankfully the cameras had stopped, and she reached for the glass of champagne that had materialized in front of her.

"I don't think I can do this." She gulped the cold champagne down, shivering as the bubbles burned her throat.

"You can, and you will."

"Please don't take this too far," she begged, her eyes pleading. He looked at her from across the table before reaching forward to clasp one of her hands in his.

"What's too far?"

"You know," she accused.

"You don't want me to take care of that ache? The one right now throbbing between your legs? You don't want me to lave you with my tongue, to suck your nipples, to kiss you until you can't breathe?"

His words kept stoking the fire he'd started

earlier. It terrified her. Because right now, she'd let him do all those things and more. And then hate herself. Forever. She'd never be able to forgive herself, and when Zak was back in his body, she was sure he wouldn't forgive her either. Even though it was his body she was responding to, their unique chemistry that had her all fired up and squirming in her chair, the fact was, it wasn't him. She shook her head, and he released her.

"Very well." He smiled as if he was utterly unaffected, but she knew by the light flush along his cheekbones and the sheen of perspiration on his forehead that his body was just as affected as hers. She wasn't going to mention it, though, because that just might push him to find his own release. Looked like they'd both be suffering blue balls tonight.

CHAPTER SIXTEEN

D inner had been delicious, and she'd surprised herself by enjoying the evening. They'd ordered a host of different dishes, and he'd teased her with food, feeding her various gastronomic delights and laughing at her reactions. She'd relished the food, delighted it was sustaining her, so she didn't feel the need for blood. It crossed the back of her mind that maybe she wasn't a vampire anymore, but she pushed the thought down. That was something to be examined later with Zak.

They'd stayed at the restaurant until late. He'd plied her with champagne and swept her around the dance floor to the sultry sounds of the jazz band. It was one of the most romantic nights of her life, and it was with the wrong man. She was silent on the elevator ride back to their floor, again keeping her gaze averted from the mirrors.

"Thank you." He spoke softly, standing by the window in their suite, looking out at the city and its twinkling lights below them.

"For what?" She moved to look out the window, keeping her distance.

"For a lovely evening. I had a good time." He sounded surprised.

She glanced at him from beneath her lashes. "I had a good time too," she admitted.

"If things were different..." He trailed off, regret in his voice.

"But they're not." With a sigh, she turned and headed to her bedroom. She slipped out of her heels and dress, leaving them in a heap on the floor, then slid beneath the covers in nothing but her panties. Pain in the side of her head reminded her to remove the hair clip, and she absently dropped it onto the bedside table before closing her eyes on a yawn.

Hours later, she stretched and yawned, wriggling back into the warm body pressed into her back. Her eyes sprung open, and she tensed. The arm draped over her waist tightened, holding her pinned to him.

"What are you doing?" she squeaked.

"Well, I was sleeping," he grumbled.

"I mean, what are you doing in my bed? Why aren't you in yours?"

He chuckled, rubbing his thumb on the flesh of her belly. "I'm not leaving you to sleep alone so you can sneak out in the middle of the night." She trembled, the weight and heat of his hand doing things to her she didn't want to think about. She tried to move away, but he pulled her back to him, his chest pressed to her shoulders. She could feel his erection pressing against her. *This was bad. This was very, very bad.*

She lay frozen, unable to move, barely breathing. Desire thrummed through her, but also fear and regret. She didn't want this. She was on edge, the pent-up desire of days spent with him with no release building to fever pitch. If he moved his hand, if he cupped her breast, she'd mount him and ride him like a cowboy. Her body was screaming at her to do it, do it, yet her mind was begging her not to, to remember he wasn't Zak, no matter how nice he was last night, how charming, attentive and romantic. He was fucking with her mind, and she hated it.

Before she could draw her next breath, he was

gone. She didn't see him move, just heard the bathroom door slam and the shower turn on. Releasing the breath she'd been holding, she sprang out of bed and quickly dressed, not caring what she wore as long as she was fully clothed before he came out.

She was pacing in the living room when a knock sounded at the door. She looked over to the bedroom door. She could still hear the shower running. Crossing the room, she opened the door to discover room service. A young man pushed a trolley into the room.

"Where would you like it?" he asked.

"Errrr."

"How about on the balcony?" he suggested, already pushing the cart toward the balcony doors.

"Uh, yeah, sure. Why not?"

He pulled the curtains back and opened the sliding doors. Pushing the trolley outside, he set up breakfast at the outside table. Georgia wandered out and leaned against the balcony railing, looking down into the city below. Guilt washed over her again that she was experiencing these things with the wrong person.

She heard the bedroom door open and close, felt Zak's presence as he joined them on the balcony.

The young man finished setting up their meal and smiled at both of them. "Enjoy your breakfast." Zak pressed notes into his hand and saw him to the door.

"Come on. Eat." He grabbed her wrist and led her to the table. She plopped into a chair and lifted the lid on the plate in front of her. A stack of pancakes drizzled in maple syrup greeted her.

"Wow." She almost drooled. How did he know it was her favorite? Scooping a forkful of pancake into her mouth, she closed her eyes as she chewed, trying to hold back the moan. They were fucking fantastic.

"Good?" Zak asked.

She didn't look up, just kept stuffing her mouth with pancake. She felt syrup dribble down her chin and wiped it away with the back of her hand, all the while not meeting his gaze. "Mmmmhmmm."

"It's very interesting." She heard his cutlery clatter on his plate, and a quick glance showed he'd finished his breakfast. She was so wrapped up in her pancakes she wasn't sure what he'd had. A hint of bacon was in the air, maybe bacon and eggs?

"What is?"

"That you haven't felt the need for blood in what? Twenty-four hours? Maybe longer."

She froze with the fork halfway to her mouth

219

and looked at him. His face was serious. She calculated back in her head. He was right: she'd last fed off the attendant in the dressing room. And that same night, she'd eaten food again. And the next day, she'd eaten food. And this morning, she was eating food. And not craving blood at all. She should be clamoring for it by now. She could have compelled the room service guy to let her take a sip, but it hadn't occurred to her. She hadn't needed to.

"Why is that?" She didn't expect him to have an answer; it was more of a rhetorical question. He shrugged, taking a mouthful of coffee. The aroma drifted over the table, and her nose twitched. Coffee. She hadn't had coffee since the time in her farmhouse when her aunt arrived. Back then, it had tasted like nothing. She used to live off the stuff in the pre-vampire days, loving the taste, the caffeine kick. She shoved the last of her pancakes into her mouth, hiding behind her hand because she'd shoved too much in and could barely chew. Swallowing, she reached for her own coffee cup and took a mouthful. *Oh, my God*. She could taste it again!

"It has to be linked to your magic," he said, watching her practically making love to her coffee cup.

"How so?"

"Not really sure, I'm just guessing, but I'd say your magic has been fighting the effects of you turning vampire, and it's slowly coming out on top."

"Fighting the effects..." Her thoughts drifted off, remembering her fever, passing out, how her injuries were scarring instead of disappearing altogether. Could he be right? It certainly sounded plausible.

"Do you think my magic could reverse me being a vampire? That I'd become human again?"

"Is that what you want?"

His question caught her off guard. *Was it what she wanted?* She knew she'd spent a long time in regret ever since Zak turned her, but with the daylight protection spell giving her back the ability to walk in the sun, that went a long way to giving her back what she wanted. A normal life. She shrugged. She'd loved her old life, but she also loved her new life with Zak. It was up to her to reconcile the two. Would reverting to human form be the solution? Especially if she had magic to protect her? She needed to have a discussion with Zak, not the hunter.

He knew the minute she shut down; she saw it in the way his lip curled in a smirk. Pushing his chair back, he got to his feet, then stopped by her chair and looked down at her. "Go visit your aunt today. Meet the coven. Do the witchy thing."

"What are you going to do?" She frowned, not trusting this sudden freedom.

"I've got things I need to take care of." With a soft kiss on her forehead, he was gone.

Georgia remained at the table, enjoying the last sips of her coffee and the early morning sun on her skin. It was still a little chilly, but the day promised to be a glorious autumn day. Finally, she pulled herself out of her daydreaming and went into the bathroom to take a shower. She'd dispensed with hygiene this morning in an effort to put distance between herself and the hunter, but now she was looking forward to standing under the waterfall spray and luxuriating in it.

Looking at her reflection in the bathroom mirror, she let out a startled shriek. Holy shit, she looked a red hot mess. Her hair was a wild nest around her head. Her mascara had streaked under her eyes and halfway down her face. *Oh, my God.* Embarrassment heated her cheeks. She'd opened the door to the room service guy looking like this. He hadn't flinched. And Zak had sat across from her and eaten breakfast, giving no clue she looked like a train wreck.

She stripped with jerky movements, leaving her clothes on the floor, and stepped beneath the spray. She'd been right: it was the best shower she'd ever had. Grabbing the loofa, she squeezed shower gel on it and scrubbed herself clean, her skin tingling and silky smooth, the scent of lavender and honeysuckle surrounding her.

She stayed under the spray way too long until her fingers were pruned. Eventually, she dragged herself out, then dried and dressed in the clothes she'd left on the floor. She found a hairdryer in the vanity unit and blasted her mane of hair, getting it mostly dry before braiding it once more, this time in a softer braid that fell forward over one shoulder, the pink peeking through the weave. Back in the bedroom, she dug the card out of the pocket of her other jeans. The Black Cauldron. Aunt Melissa had said it was a couple of streets away.

She'd been delaying the inevitable. She needed to get her head back in the game, to meet with the witches and get this mess sorted. Sitting around having decadent breakfasts and luxurious showers were not going to help anything, and a twinge of guilt colored her cheeks.

Downstairs she asked the concierge for directions. Sure enough, it was literally only two streets away. Although the concierge had frowned at the name, saying he'd never heard of it, he did know the address typed in black beneath it. Thanking him, she set off and stood outside a quaint shop ten minutes later.

The shop front reminded her of something out of a Harry Potter novel. This place would have been right at home in Diagon Alley with its wooden-framed windows, displayed with wands, cauldrons, books stacked sky-high. Smiling in anticipation, Georgia pushed the door open, and a bell jangled over her head announcing her arrival.

The shop smelled...interesting—a mixture of incense, herbs, and old books. It was a little heady. It made her want to throw open some windows to get some fresh air. The wooden floorboards beneath her feet creaked as she moved further into the store, spied a counter painted purple with gold lettering around the frame...she couldn't make out the language.

"Can I help you?" A woman appeared from behind a curtain that presumably led to a storeroom or some such place. Biting the inside of her cheek to keep from laughing, Georgia eyed the woman with curly orange hair heading her way. She was dressed in the most psychedelic pair of pants Georgia had ever seen and a bright purple tank top that revealed she wasn't wearing a bra. She was several pounds overweight, and Georgia pegged her to be at least sixty.

"Errr. I'm looking for my aunt? Melissa Foster?"

The woman shrieked so loudly Georgia clamped her hands over her ears. "You must be Georgia!" She scrambled around the counter and wrapped Georgia in a bear hug, "We've been waiting for you."

The woman's orange fuzzy head reached Georgia's collarbone, and she looked down at her, half in fright, half in delight. "Am I late? Sorry." She wheezed, unable to draw a decent breath with the small round woman squeezing the life out of her.

"Oh, sorry." She released her, stepped back, and eyed her up and down. That's when Georgia noticed the other woman was barefoot, and each toenail was painted a different color.

"I'm Tilda. I own this place. Welcome."

"This is...amazing."

"Tilda, I could hear your screeching from upstairs. Is Georgia here?" Melissa appeared from behind the curtain. "Finally!" She huffed when her eyes landed on Georgia.

"Sorry, Aunt Melissa." The two women hugged, then Melissa held her at arm's length, her hands resting on Georgia's shoulders as she peered intently at her.

"Your magic has grown." She nodded in satisfaction.

"How can you tell?"

"I can feel it. And your aura has changed. Come on, let's head upstairs. Some of the girls are already here. The others will join us soon."

"Are you doing the spell today?" Georgia followed her behind the curtain, which revealed a small annex and a staircase. She followed her aunt up, praying the wood would hold as it creaked and groaned beneath their weight.

"No. We need the power of the full moon. Tomorrow night."

On the next floor was a large open space with several pentagrams painted on the floor and workbenches placed around the outside of the room. Large floor cushions were scattered around. The ceiling was painted black with what looked like stars dotted throughout.

"This is where we meet, practice and workshop." Melissa gestured with her arm. "And this is Kathryn, Franny, and Vida."

Three women had been huddled around a bench at the back of the room but looked up when they heard Melissa. They closed the book they'd been hunched over and, smiling, walked toward Georgia, arms outstretched.

"I'm Vida." Vida was all limbs and towered over Georgia by at least a foot. Her hair was twisted on top of her head in a neat bun, and she wore pressed jeans complete with a crease down the center of each leg and a buttoned-up soft lemon cardigan. She looked too young to be dressed like a librarian.

"I'm Kathryn." Kathryn looked mid-forties, her mousy hair cut in a flattering pixie cut. She dressed like the CEO of a very important company, complete with powerful red lipstick that matched her stilettoes.

"I'm Franny." Franny's dreadlocked hair fell to her waist in a riot of color, with feathers and beads woven into it, so it clicked and clacked each time she moved her head. She wore jeans with so many tears in them they barely qualified as jeans and a stained T-shirt that had definitely seen better days. Like Tilda downstairs, her feet were bare, but her toenails were all one color. Black.

"Hi." Georgia hugged them all back and prayed she'd remember their names.

"Welcome to the coven." Franny grinned, bouncing from foot to foot.

"I'm in the coven?"

"Not yet. We're holding an initiation ceremony to bring you in, but it's a done deal."

"An initiation ceremony?"

"Nothing to worry about, sweetheart," Melissa wrapped an arm around her shoulder and gave her a squeeze. "We have to officially bring you into the coven so your magic can merge with ours."

"Okaaaaay. When?"

"Once everyone is here. Tilda will be contacting the rest of the coven now, letting them know you're here."

"So we don't need the full moon for this?"

Melissa shook her head, "No. We draw power from the moon, stars, earth whenever it's needed. We don't abuse our power, and we don't channel from other sources unless we really, really need to. An initiation ceremony doesn't require any of that."

Franny grabbed her hand and smiled in delight. "It's so great you're here. Mel tells us you're a vampire *and* a witch!"

"I'm guessing that's unusual?"

"It's unheard of. You're unique."

"Oh." Melissa had downplayed the whole witch-vampire thing, especially when Zak had said it was impossible.

"Come and tell me all about it. How did you become a vampire? And this man of yours? Mel tells us he's super-hot." Franny dragged her over to a pile of cushions. Georgia went willingly, sinking down next to the younger woman whose energy and enthusiasm was contagious.

Georgia and Franny spent the next hour exchanging stories. Georgia liked her. Franny told her she was nineteen and in college. She was studying to be a teacher. She'd discovered her magical abilities as a child, and her hippy mother had embraced them, encouraging her to use her magic, to let it grow and expand. Franny had joined the coven as soon as she'd turned eighteen. However, she'd been a frequent visitor to The Black Cauldron for years, buying ingredients for her spells, joining workshops, and just hanging out.

As they'd talked, the room had begun to fill up. Georgia counted ten women, plus herself. The entire coven was here. Georgia couldn't help the sudden pang of anxiety that shot through her. Her aunt approached and held out a hand. Georgia placed hers in it and allowed herself to be pulled to her feet.

"Come. We must prepare." Melissa led her

across the room to the stairs leading up. Georgia followed dutifully.

"Prepare how?" she asked when they stepped onto the small landing that held nothing but a closed door. Melissa opened the door and led Georgia into an apartment. This must be where Tilda lived. Georgia remembered her aunt telling her the witch lived above her store.

"You must be cleansed and wear a robe." Melissa moved into the bathroom and flicked on the bathtub faucet. She withdrew a bag of...something...from her pocket and sprinkled it into the water.

"While you're in the bath, I need you to meditate, to open your chakras."

Georgia nodded. She remembered her aunt talking about chakras before. Although admittedly she hadn't paid a whole lot of attention, she'd give it her best shot. If she could get her mind to shut up for five minutes and allow her to meditate.

Melissa left the room, returning a moment later with a white robe. "After your bath, dry yourself and put this on. Nothing else. You must be naked beneath it, no restriction. Leave your hair loose."

"Okay."

Melissa closed the door, and Georgia stripped, easing herself into the hot bath. Submerging herself up to her neck, she closed her eyes and did her best to become Zen. She wasn't sure if it worked or not, but Melissa must have sensed something since she soon knocked on the door and told her to get out of the bath and into the robe.

The robe was more of a caftan than a robe, flowing to her wrists and ankles. She opened the door to find Melissa standing waiting, dressed in an identical robe, only black.

"Come." Clasping Georgia's hand, she led her back downstairs. Georgia glanced around to see the other women clad in the same black robes as her aunt.

"Witches! Please, form a circle," Tilda called out. She stood at one of the pentagrams painted on the floor. Obediently the women took their places, pulling the hoods of their robes up over their heads. "You too, Georgia. Come here by me." Georgia moved to stand next to Tilda, whom she assumed was the coven leader. What do you even call the leader? Head witch? She'd have to remember to ask.

"Before we begin, let me introduce you to everyone. I know you've met some of the girls, but clockwise we have Jennifer, Kathryn, Franny, Vida, Karylin, Livy, Roanna, Crista, and Melissa." Georgia smiled weakly. There was no way in hell she would remember who was who.

"First, we're going to cast a circle," Tilda began. "A circle represents unity, accord, wholeness, and a safe space where we can all find comfort and protection. We call on the four elements—air, fire, water, and earth—and we map them to direction, so air is east, fire is south, water is west, the earth is north." Georgia nodded. She recalled her aunt casting the circles for them when they practiced at the farmhouse.

"When we've finished spell casting, we must release the space. So today, we'll cast the circle, welcome you into the coven, and then release the circle. Okay?"

All the witches nodded, so Georgia followed suit. Even though Tilda had explained what was happening, she still didn't truly understand. Franny winked at her and grinned. "Just go along with it," she mouthed. Georgia smiled back and gave a slight nod. *Okay*.

Tilda began. "Hold hands, please." Once everyone had clasped hands, she closed her eyes, took a deep breath, blowing it out through her mouth. "Beings of Air, Guardians of the East, Breath of Transformation—Come! Be welcome in this sacred space. We ask that you stand firm to guard, protect, refresh, and motivate. Support the magic created here by conveying our wishes on every wind as it reaches across the Earth."

Kathryn spoke next. "Beings of Fire, Guardians of the South, Spark of Creation that banished the darkness—Come! Be welcome in this sacred space. We ask that you stand firm to guard, protect, activate, and fulfill. Support the magic created here by conveying our wishes to the sun, the stars, and every beam of light as it embraces the Earth.

Karylin was next. "Beings of Water, Guardians of the West, Rain of Inspiration— Come! Be welcome in this sacred space. We ask that you stand firm to guard, protect, heal, and nurture. Support the magic created here by conveying our wishes to dewdrops and waves as they wash across the world."

Then it was Roanna. "Being of Earth, Guardians of the North, Soil of Foundation— Come! Be welcome in this sacred space. We ask that you stand firm to guard, protect, mature, and provide. Support the magic created here by conveying our wishes to every grain of sand, every bit of loam that is our world."

Tilda spoke once more. "The circle is cast. We are between the worlds, beyond the bounds of time and space where night and day, birth and death, joy and sorrow meet as one."

Georgia wasn't sure what to expect, a gust of wind, a power surge of some sort, a clap of thunder, but absolutely nothing happened. Nothing that she could see, hear, or sense anyway. The witches let go of each other's hands, and Tilda turned to her.

"Georgia, please stand in the center." Tilda handed her a book, already open. "We shall guide you through the ceremony, but you'll see the full instructions on the pages in front of you. Are you ready?"

"I guess." She didn't know but felt she was in too deep to back out now. Glancing at the book, she scanned the words. Seemed harmless enough, no blood sacrifices, no cutting the heads off chickens. She sucked in a deep breath and blew it out, reading from the book.

"Goddess of the moon, come to me this day." She could hear movement around her, noticed as the witches discreetly placed an altar in front of her with several items on it. They returned to their places in the circle, and Georgia continued.

"I am here to consecrate myself in your name." Placing the book on the altar, she stood with her arms held up, palms pointing outward.

"We have cast this circle this day to perform the act of dedication of my mind, body, and spirit to the Lady, her consort, and to the religion and science of Witchcraft. From this day forward, I will honor and respect both the divine and myself. I will hold two perfect words in my heart: perfect love and perfect trust. I vow to honor the path I have chosen, the divine, and myself."

She raised her right palm outstretched to the ceiling. "I vow to hold the ideology of the Craft in my heart and my mind for the totality of this lifetime and beyond."

She opened her palm toward the floor. "Blessed be my feet; may they always walk the path of the eternal and divine light."

She placed both hands over her heart. "Blessed be my heart that it may beat steady and true. May the warmth of my love spread throughout the galaxy."

Placing her fingertips to her lips, she said, "Blessed be my lips that they shall utter truth and purity of mind and soul. May wisdom flow for the benefit of all humankind."

Her hands moved to her lower belly, above her womb. "Blessed be my womb that holds and produces the creation of the human essence. I vow to guide, protect, and teach the children of the world."

Her fingers rose to her forehead. "Blessed be my astral sight, that I may see through the veil of life with the truth of the divine."

She picked up the small silver bell from the altar and rang it seven times. Then she picked up a white cord and wrapped it firmly around her hand. Picking up a small ceremonial knife, she held it in the same hand. "I, Georgia, in the presence of the universe, and my sisters of the coven, do of my own free will and mind, most solemnly swear that I will ever abide by the religion and science of the Craft. From this day, I shall honor, respect, and cherish this oath I have taken." With trembling fingers, she unwound the cord and returned it to the altar. Picking up the bell again, she rang it nine times. She picked up a chalice, careful not to spill its contents as her hands continued to shake. Holding the chalice up high, she repeated the words from the book.

"With the partaking of this wine, I take into my body that of the Goddess and seal my oath...forever." She drank half the wine, trying not to grimace, as red wine was not her thing.

She held the chalice aloft again, saying, "Accept this wine as my offering of thanksgiving," then returned it to the altar. She picked up a plate holding a chunk of bread.

"As grain is the bounty of the Goddess, and the eating of it denotes the sacrifice of the Lord and his rebirth, I seal my oath forever as I take into my body that of the consort!" She took a bite of the bread before returning the plate to the altar.

"I wish to thank the Lord and Lady for presiding over this ritual and my sisters welcoming me into this coven. May we together walk within the light, forever." Silence descended and lasted for several heartbeats.

Roanna's voice in the silence made her jump. "Guardians, Guides, and Ancestors of the North and Earth, we thank you for your presence and protection. Keep us rooted in your rich soil, so our spirits grow steadily until we return to your protection again. Hail and farewell."

Karylin was next. "Guardians, Guides, and Ancestors of the West and Water, we thank you for your presence and protection. Keep us flowing ever toward wholeness in body, mind, and spirit until we return to your protection again. Hail and farewell."

Kathryn spoke up. "Guardians, Guides, and Ancestors of the South and Fire, we thank you for your presence and protection. Keep your fires ever burning within our soul to light up any darkness and drive it away until we return to your protection again. Hail and farewell."

Then it was back to Tilda. "Guardians, Guides, and Ancestors of the East and Air, we thank you for your presence and protection. Keep your winds blowing fresh with ideas and hopefulness until we return to your protection again. Hail and farewell." Tilda stepped forward. Standing beside Georgia, she clasped her hand. "Great Spirit, thank you for blessing this space. We know that a part of you is always with us, as a still small voice that guides and nurtures. Help us to listen to that voice, to trust it, and trust in our magic. Merry meet, merry part, and merry meet again."

With the circle open, the witches surrounded her in hugs and congratulations, welcoming her into the fold. The candles were extinguished, and the lights turned back on—Georgia hadn't even noticed the candlelight; she'd been so engrossed in the ceremony.

"You did great." Franny hugged her.

"Thanks. Am I meant to feel...different?"

Franny laughed. "Not particularly! It wasn't spell casting as such, just a ceremony to welcome you into the coven. Not every coven does it, and not all witches belong to covens; some choose to work alone."

"Really?" Georgia followed Franny over to where she'd stacked her clothes on top of her bags, averting her eyes when Franny shrugged out of her robe, leaving her naked.

"There's no hard and fast rules. Witchcraft is cool like that. You can take what you want from it."

Georgia excused herself to return to the apartment upstairs, don her own clothes, and rebraid her hair. She'd have to ask why they used ceremonial robes, why they needed to have nothing binding on their bodies. She had so much to learn.

Many of the witches dispersed after the ceremony. With jobs to go back to, they couldn't hang around. Tilda served up herbal tea, a purple concoction that was truly revolting. Georgia choked it down, not wanting to be rude. Soon it was only Melissa, Tilda, Franny, and herself. Georgia crossed to the towering bookcases at the back of the room. They were jammed with a multitude of books— some looked ancient, some looked like they were fresh off the printing press.

"What are you looking for?" Franny asked.

"Nothing in particular," she told her. It was better if the witches didn't know what she was up to, for as welcoming and friendly as they had been, she felt something was a little off, a little dark, a little unwelcoming. She couldn't put her finger on what, exactly, and she didn't know who she could trust. So she kept her mouth shut.

"There's tons of great stuff here," Franny told her, her face bright, her cheeks flushed. "Anything you want to know, just ask. I've got a class in a couple of hours, so I'm going to meditate for a bit, try and settle myself after all the excitement. I still feel wired."

"Nothing to do with all that herbal tea, was it?" Georgia teased.

Franny laughed. "Could be, could be." She moved to a spot beneath the window where the sun streamed through, maneuvered a floor cushion, and made herself comfortable.

Georgia waited until she was sure Franny had zoned out, then returned to the books. Her aunt and Tilda had returned to the shop downstairs, leaving her alone. It seemed strange that they kept brushing her off when she asked about the spell they were working on, but she'd shrugged it off. She probably wouldn't understand it anyway.

Running her fingers along the spines of the books, she recalled Melissa telling her to take away another witch's magic was considered dark magic. Black magic. No books leaped out at her proclaiming to be a beginner's guide to black magic, and she guessed she wouldn't find such a book here. Not in plain sight. Instead, she pulled down a selection, three old tombs that looked promising and three more recent ones. Carrying her haul to a workbench, she settled in, pushing the newer books to one side. She didn't expect to find anything in them; she'd chosen them as a cover in case anyone asked what she was doing.

The three older books she'd chosen had no titles. Their covers appeared to be old leather. One of them had two catches keeping the pages closed, another had a silver pentagram embedded in the cover, and the third was a plain brown cover with no embellishments at all. She chose that one first.

Flipping it open, the smell of old parchment, dust, and—was that lavender?—reached her nose. The pages were yellowed, the writing faint, only just readable. She couldn't begin to guess how old this book might be since it looked handwritten. Like her aunt's grimoire, it had diagrams to assist in identifying various plants, stones, and tools for witchcraft.

"You've been engrossed in those books for

hours." Her aunt's voice startled her. Glancing up, Georgia saw it was dark outside. She looked over to where Franny was meditating; only the cushion was empty. She hadn't heard her leave.

"They are fascinating," Georgia admitted. The book with the clasps holding it closed had turned out to be an encyclopedia on all the supernatural creatures. Not only vampires, witches, and werewolves, but trolls, fairies, gargoyles, dragons. Creatures she'd never imagined to be real, but according to this book, they all existed. Sadly she'd found nothing that would help her break the hunter's connection to his magic.

"Are you ready for tomorrow?"

"I guess so. I just wish I knew more about the spell. What will it do? What's going to happen?"

"All in due course, my dear. You should go. Get some rest. Tomorrow is going to be a big day, and we need you at full strength."

"Oh. Okay." She hadn't been expecting her aunt to kick her out, had thought they'd spend more time together, that she'd teach her more of her witchcraft heritage. Melissa helped her return the books to the shelves, then hugged her.

"Come back tomorrow night. At dusk."

"Can I come back sooner? I'd like to keep reading." She indicated the bookshelves behind her.

Melissa shook her head. "Tilda and I will be prepping for the spell. And it's best you rest. Don't practice any magic tomorrow at all. You need to be fully charged, so to speak. We're going to have to channel your power. If you deplete yourself beforehand, the spell might fail."

"Okay. Well, I'll see you tomorrow night then." She thought it strange they wouldn't let her return until it was time for the spell, even stranger that no one would tell her about this new mysterious spell. Precisely what would it do? They said it would kill the hunter, but not how. Worry pulled at her. She was keeping secrets from everyone, and it appeared they were all keeping secrets from her too.

CHAPTER SEVENTEEN

W ith a final hug at the door to the shop, Georgia stepped out into the night. She was almost back to the hotel when she passed a trendy little pub. Backing up, she peered inside. She was hungry and could use a drink, so why not? For a woman who was used to her own space and own company, she hadn't been alone in a long time, and she welcomed it. Stepping inside, she let her eyes adjust to the dim light for a moment before stepping up to the bar. It was early; not many patrons filled the small space. Grabbing a menu at the bar, she ordered a burger and a beer and found herself a seat in a booth made for four.

"Here you are." Zak slid into the booth opposite her. Her mouth full of burger, she looked at him. He didn't seem angry, which was a relief. She finished chewing and swallowed.

"I was hungry," she said a tad defensively. Why did she have to justify herself to him anyway?

"Is it good?" He indicated the burger.

"It's fucking brilliant!" She grinned. She took another bite, watched as he headed to the bar, returning with two bottles of beer.

"Have a good day?" he asked conversationally, taking a swig.

"What is this?" She frowned, suspicious.

"What's what?"

"What you're doing? Being nice. Why aren't you pissed that I didn't come straight back to the hotel?"

"Is that why you came here? To piss me off?"

"Actually, no. I came in because I was hungry and could use a drink. Or two."

He nodded. "That's what I thought."

"So, you're not angry?"

"Nope." He took another swig of beer, watching her. She held his gaze for a moment longer before shrugging and picking up her burger again, taking a massive bite and closing her eyes as the flavor burst over her tongue.

His own burger arrived shortly after, and they ate in silence. Finally, when the plates were cleared away, and he'd ordered them both a whiskey, he asked the question she'd been hoping to avoid.

"How was your day with the witches?"

She didn't know what to tell him. Of her suspicion that they were keeping something from her. Because he was the enemy. She didn't know if the witches were her enemy too, and she wished she had *her* Zak here to talk to.

Blowing out a breath, she muttered, "It was okay."

"Just okay?" One dark brow arched.

"I'm part of their coven now," she admitted.

"You don't seem happy about it," he observed.

"I don't know...it's just...only a few months ago I was human, then I became a vampire, now I'm a witch—hell, I don't even know if I'm a vampire anymore! I don't know what I am."

"You're more powerful than you know. Than you can imagine." His dark eyes pinned her to her seat.

"And what the fuck does that mean? You all talk so vaguely without giving me details." She cursed, jaw tense.

"I can't tell you. It's too risky."

"Risky for you, you mean."

"Exactly." He smirked at her, the curl of his lip drawing her attention.

"If you keep staring at me like that, we're going to be in a whole lot of trouble you hadn't counted on," he ground out. She could hear it in his voice. His desire. Tearing her eyes away, she slid from the booth, stopping when his hand snaked around her wrist.

"Where are you going?"

"To the bar. I'm pre-loading for tomorrow." She tugged out of his grip.

Cocking his head, he frowned. "Pre-loading?"

"Tomorrow's a full moon, right? Something big is going down, and I'm smack dab in the middle of it. What better way to face your demons than laden with alcohol?"

"Sounds like a plan." He stood, captured her hand with his, and led her to the bar. She eyed him in shock.

"What are you doing?" The change in him confused her, even more so when he opened up a tab at the bar, pulled a bar stool up next to hers, and ordered shots.

"Having fun?"

"Fun?"

"This is the most fun I think we can have...with our clothes on. Unless you want to go back to the hotel and...?"

"What? No! This is great. This is my kinda fun."

He laughed out loud, clinked his glass with hers, and downed the shot. Signaling the bartender, he told him to leave the bottle.

Three hours later and she was well and truly hammered. Maybe she wasn't a vampire anymore because she sure as shit wasn't burning off alcohol like she used to. The room was not precisely spinning, more like swaying. All her worries had taken flight on an alcohol-fueled plane to who the hell cared.

"I need to pee," she slurred, sliding off her stood and almost face-planting. Since when did the floor get so far away?

"Easy there." Zak laughed, catching her, holding her steady until she got her feet under her. "Need a hand?"

"Nope. I've been peeing on my own since I was born. But thank you." Weaving across the room, she banged through the ladies' room door, nearly clocking herself in the face when the door slammed against the wall and bounced back at her. "Ooops."

Sitting on the toilet, she smiled. She was having fun. She'd missed nights like this. Drinking at the bar. Having Zak with her kept the sleazes away, which in turn stopped her from having to punch some dickhead in the face. She didn't want to think about the witches. Or the hunter. Or Skye. Or any of it. God, life was so goddamn complicated, and tonight, she wanted to be free. And she was.

"Zakky!" She sidled up to him at the bar, leaning into him. He smiled, shaking his head at her. His eyes had followed her from the moment she'd opened the bathroom door and weaved her way back to the bar. Several men had looked like they were going to approach, but he'd stared them down.

"Zakky?" He laughed.

"What?" She frowned.

"You called me Zakky."

"No, I didn't."

"You did."

"Get me a drink."

"How about water?"

"Pft. How about...tequila? Cos, y'know, this might be my last night on Earth!" she declared dramatically, waving her arm in the air and staggering. Slipping his arm around her waist, he heaved her back onto the bar stool by his side.

"Y'know"—she looked at him—"I can't work you out."

"Oh?"

"You're this big bad hunter that the witches are

terrified of, I'm on your hit list, yet you're being nice to me."

"I didn't think you wanted to talk about that tonight," he reminded her.

"You're right!" she suddenly yelled, making him jump. "Ssssh," she shushed him with a finger over her lips. "You're being too loud." He laughed, shaking his head.

It was two in the morning, the bar was packed, yet they stayed. When a song came on the jukebox that she liked, she dragged him up to dance with her. Her sense of rhythm was totally off, and he did little but shuffle from one foot to the other, but still, she beamed at him, delighted. Another hour passed. They lost their seats at the bar, but he found them a spot to sit and catch their breath. Only he didn't appear to be drunk or breathless.

"Phew! It's warm in here." She'd shrugged out of her hoodie and draped it over the back of her chair, where it promptly fell to the floor because she'd missed. He picked it up and placed it on his chair.

"Do you have any friends?" she asked, leaning her elbows on the table and her chin in her hands.

"No."

"That's sad." She smiled sadly at him, then tears

filled her eyes. "Geez, that's really sad, man." She sniffed.

"Hey," he soothed, leaning over to wipe a tear from her cheek, "it's okay."

"You're okay? I don't feel so good." She lowered her head to rest her cheek on the table.

"Ready to go?" He chuckled, crouching by her side.

"I want to plant cats."

"Plant cats?"

"Mmmm. They're so cute. Scratchy little bastards, though."

"Do you have a cat?"

"No." Her eyes closed, and she was out.

CHAPTER EIGHTEEN

"Georgia!" Zak smiled at her, his eyes sparkling, his arms reaching for her.

"What's going on? Why are you here?" She held out a hand to ward him off. She'd had enough of the hunter's games, using her own desires against her.

"What? What do you mean?"

"Just cut the crap, okay? I'm tired of all this." She sat down on the edge of the bed they shared. It was cruel of him to choose this setting.

"Georgia?" He kneeled in front of her, brows pulling together. "What's happened? The last thing I remember is going after the hunter. I don't know what he did, but something hit me like a massive electric shot. I remember *my whole body seizing. That's it. That's all I've got. What's happened? Why are we here?"*

"Zak?" She cupped his face, searching his eyes. Was it really him? Her Zak?

"It's me." His voice was soft, reassuring. Could it really be? She was hesitant to believe, to trust that the hunter would allow them this...with trembling fingers, she traced his face before tugging him to her. Before their lips met, he froze. "Who else would it be?" He frowned, his breath hot on her face.

"What?" she murmured, already lost in the heat swirling between them.

"You asked if it was me. Who else would it be?" He pulled back, but she refused to let him go.

"No one. It doesn't matter." She planted her mouth on his, poured all of her pent-up emotion into this kiss. He responded immediately, tongue dueling with hers...

"Oh my God," she whimpered, grasping his broad shoulders and pressing into him.

"You taste so good," he whispered, running his tongue along her earlobe, muttering against her skin what he wanted to do to her...with her. He ran his lips over her jaw and back to the corner of her mouth. Threading her hands through his thick black hair, she cupped the back of his neck and pulled his lips to hers. He teased her mouth with the tip of his tongue, licking along

her lower lip before he slanted his mouth across hers and turned her to jelly.

His mouth and teeth traveled down her body, leaving a trail of fire in their wake. She barely noticed when he tugged her shirt over her head and unhooked her bra, freeing her breasts. He stopped, mesmerized. His eyes were hooded with desire, and she sucked in a breath, arching her back. She wanted him to touch her. Needed him to touch her. His mouth descended to one aching breast; he took her nipple into his mouth and drew long and hard. He divided his attention between each breast equally, licking and nipping until she was squirming against him.

They tumbled back onto the bed, her legs wrapping around his hips, and he groaned into her mouth as his hands cupped her behind, pulling her impossibly closer. He shuddered as she dragged her mouth from his to explore his neck, tracing circles with her tongue, tasting him, teasing him. His breath hitched as she scraped his neck with her teeth, but she didn't bite him. Not yet. If she bit him now, it'd be all over, and she'd waited too long for this.

His hands were all over her, tugging at her jeans, pulling them down her legs until she was naked beneath him. Burying his face in her neck, he nipped.

"You're so fucking delicious," he said as his lips and

teeth explored the curve of her throat, down to her collarbone. His hand slid down her body, reaching with his fingers between her legs. He groaned when he felt how wet she was, rubbing in circular motions until she bucked against his hand, moaned his name, and raked her nails down his back.

"Jesus. So hot. So wet. Mine." He growled, capturing her mouth at the same time he buried two fingers deep inside her. His tongue matched the rhythm of his fingers, and her body jerked and tightened around him. He muttered incoherent words into her mouth as she came apart in his arms.

"My turn." She pushed him off her and onto his back. Propping herself on one elbow, she let her eyes devour him, his broad shoulders, chiseled chest, rock hard abs, to his erection standing tall and proud. Straddling him, she worked her way down his body, dropping kisses along the way until her mouth was right where she wanted it. He was frozen beneath her, body tense, as she flicked her tongue out and circled the swollen head of his cock. He groaned and twisted his fingers in her hair as she worked him with her mouth, sliding up and down, running her tongue over and around him.

"Georgia, stop!" he hissed, pulling her off him. "I need to be inside you. Now!" He flipped them, tossing her

to the mattress and moving between her legs in one fluid movement.

"Open your eyes," Zak commanded. "Look at me."

She did. They watched each other as he entered her, slowly pushing into her as she stretched and adjusted to the size of him. He paused, then withdrew with agonizing slowness. Her hips bucked, trying to draw him back into her, but he held firm, his fingers digging into her hips to hold her still.

"Please..." she groaned,

"What do you want?" he teased, rocking slightly, teasing her with his cock.

"I want you." Another groan, laced with frustration

"You want me to fuck you?"

"Yes!"

With a quick deep thrust, he buried himself completely inside her. Her body convulsed around his, and she cried out. He started slow and steady, but her writhing and bucking beneath him pushed him over the edge. Before she knew it, he was pounding into her with a force and speed that would have killed her if she was still human. Instead, she met every thrust with joyful abandon.

She wrapped her legs around his waist, giving him deeper access. He growled his approval. She sucked his tongue into her mouth and gripped him inside her with *a force that sent shock waves rippling through her body and shudders to rock his. Moments before her orgasm hit, his teeth sunk into her neck, and he drank from her as she exploded around him, milking him with her internal muscles until he tore his mouth from her and threw back his head with a roar, his own orgasm consuming him.*

She woke with a groan and a throbbing head. As hot and satisfying as the dream walk with Zak had been, the reality of one very hung-over body overshadowed everything.

"Here." A glass of water appeared on the bedside table, two white pills next to it.

"Thanks." Sitting up, she gingerly swung her legs out of bed, not caring that she only wore her bra and panties, that he'd obviously undressed her the night before. Right now, she needed to pee. And possibly throw up because now she was upright, the room was spinning alarmingly.

"You look a little green," Zak commented. She glanced at him. She felt more than a little green. She felt disgusting.

"Oh, God." Feeling bile rise in her throat, she rushed to the bathroom, hand clamped over her mouth. Skidding to her knees, she heaved into the toilet. She felt her hair being held back as she continued to wretch until her stomach must surely be empty. Resting her head on the arm she had draped over the toilet, she closed her eyes. She felt like shit. She was shaking and sweating.

Zak let go of her hair, and she heard the shower turn on. Then she was being lifted and shoved beneath the spray, underwear and all. She stood beneath the water, not moving until eventually she pried her eyes open and looked at Zak, who was leaning against the frame.

"Better?"

"Urgh."

He laughed, passing her a toothbrush. "Use it. You'll feel better."

Dutifully she stood in the shower and brushed her teeth. After a few minutes, he reached in and flicked the taps off, wrapping her in a big fluffy towel.

"You wanna takes these off, or shall I?" He indicated her wet bra and panties.

"I'll do it," she muttered. Wriggling under the towel, there was a wet slap as her bra hit the tiles, followed by her panties. Secure in the towel, she cautiously made her way back into the bedroom, sat on the end of the bed, and released a shaky breath. When he sat behind her, the mattress dipped, then he rubbed a towel over her wet hair. She didn't have the energy to argue with him, simply sat passively while he dried her hair, then ran a comb through it.

He finished with her hair, appearing in front of her again with the glass of water and pills from her nightstand.

"Take these. Get back into bed and sleep it off. You'll feel better."

She accepted the glass, swallowed the pills, and crawled beneath the covers still wrapped in the towel. She thought she felt his lips on her forehead but couldn't be sure, oblivion calling her.

"HEY, SLEEPYHEAD." Zak nudged her awake. She rolled over, glancing at the window and the dim light outside.

"What time is it?"

"Six o'clock."

"In the morning?" Jesus, why was he waking her up this early?

"In the evening."

"What?" *Shit*. She had to get to The Black Cauldron. Melissa had told her to come at dusk. It was dusk now. Sitting up, she was relieved that the room didn't spin.

"Did I sleep all day?"

"Yup. You were awake briefly this morning. Do you remember?"

"Throwing my guts up and showering in my underwear. Yes, I do." She paused, eyeing him. "Thank you for taking care of me. That couldn't have been pleasant."

He shrugged. Turning his back, he left the room, closing the door quietly behind him. She tossed back the covers and quickly dressed with no time to think. Her hair was a mess. She'd gone to sleep with it damp, and now it was a massive tangle around her head. Pulling her brush through it, she winced at the knots but kept going anyway, ignoring the hair ripping from her scalp with each stroke. Finally tangle-free, she braided it and slipped on her jacket.

Zak was waiting in the living room. Gone was the warm, friendly face from last night. In its place, an icy stranger. This was it. Tonight it was all going down. She hadn't found anything to break his connection with his magic, had wasted today sleeping off her hangover, and now she was out of time. Whatever spell the witches had concocted had better work—her sister's life and Zak's lay in the balance.

They stood silently, eyeing each other.

"You should go," he said.

"I...I don't know what to say," she admitted, choking.

"Why say anything?"

"Because I can feel that this is the end. I don't know what it is the end of, just that it is. And as much as I hate you for what you've done, you could have—"

He held up a hand, cutting her off, the lip curl back.

"There's still time." He sneered, his insinuation clear. And boom, he was back to being an asshole. It made it easier to leave. Striding across the room, she let herself out, half expecting him to call her back, to say he was sorry...for everything. He didn't.

She jogged to The Black Cauldron, trying not to think of the evening ahead, the trepidation building within her. Memories of Veronica surfaced, how it had felt to kill her, shame burning in her chest. She didn't want the hunter dead. Just stopped. Somehow she didn't think the witches were on the same page as her.

Tilda was waiting at the shop door for her.

"We thought maybe you'd changed your mind." Her gaze was stern, accusing.

"Nope. Slept in. Hungover."

Franny overhead and came bounding toward them. "You pulled an all-nighter?" Her voice was laced with admiration.

"Not exactly an *all*-nighter, but yeah, it was a big night. And an even bigger headache this morning." Georgia winced, remembering throwing up, the hunter holding her hair back. Classy.

"Maybe we can go for drinks tonight after this is all over." She looked at Georgia with puppy dog eyes, all big and pleading.

"Franny. You have better things to be doing than planning your social life," Tilda admonished, voice cold. "Go get ready. We need to begin."

Chastised, Franny hurried off. Tilda tossed a white robe at Georgia. "Change into that."

Figuring Tilda was still pissed at her for being late, Georgia carried the robe upstairs to the apartment. Slipping into the bathroom for privacy, she stripped and donned the robe. She waited by the stairs for the rest of the witches to join her, then followed them up the stairs to the rooftop.

NINETEEN

The women gathered around the pentagram painted on the concrete surface on the roof. The light breeze ruffled the long hooded robes they wore. Each witch held either a red candle with black symbols printed on it or a black candle with red symbols. Georgia hadn't seen the symbols before; each candle was different as far as she could tell. She was puzzling over the designs when Melissa nudged her toward the pentagram.

"Stand in the middle."

She moved to the center of the pentagram. The witches formed a complete circle around it, placing their candles in front of them on the boundary line of the pentagram. They then clasped hands.

"What do I do?" Georgia asked, jumping slightly when the candles flared to life.

"We're going to channel your magic to make us stronger," Melissa said. "You just need to relax and not fight it. Let your magic flow."

"Okay. But...can't we be seen out here?" She glanced at the taller buildings around them. If someone were to glance out of their window and see the witches gathering on the rooftop, would they call the cops?

"The building is warded. No one can see us. We're perfectly safe here."

"Oh. Okay."

It was eerie on the rooftop. The witches began chanting, and the lights around them dimmed, all except for the flames on the candles. It was weird as if suddenly they weren't in the middle of a city but miles away from civilization in the black of night. While the light breeze moved the cloaks around the witches' legs, the candles burned strong, flames not moving or bending to the wind's will.

"*Luna bohyne sorores a ja, sine nam cerpat sacrificio nos ad silu obeti, et suas magie ingressus.*" The chant became louder.

Georgia felt a tingling sensation in her feet that swept up her legs and her entire body. She sucked in a breath, then remembered her aunt's words. They were channeling her magic. She had to relax and let it flow. She blew out her breath and forced herself to relax.

"*Luna bohyne sorores a ja, sine nam cerpat sacrificio nos ad silu obeti, et suas magie ingressus. Luna bohyne sorores a ja, sine nam cerpat sacrificio nos ad silu obeti, et suas magie ingressus.*" The chanting continued, louder and louder. She strained to understand the words but couldn't make out the spell the witches were using. It didn't sound at all familiar from the things she'd read in her aunt's grimoire.

A gust of wind swirled around her, whipping around her legs, tugging at her robe, and whipping her hair around her head.

She noticed the wind was only affecting her, a mini storm within the pentagram. The chanting was louder now, yet she still couldn't make out the words. The wind was tugging at her painfully, and she felt strange, like gravity was about to lose its grip on the earth, and she just might fly up into the sky.

Around her, a beam of light began to glow, encasing her body. Every molecule began to hum; it was almost as if someone were holding a giant magnet over her head, and everything was moving up. The hum intensified, turning into more of a zap. An uncomfortable zap. This was starting to hurt. They didn't warn her it would hurt.

Pushing her hair out of her face, she looked at the witches and gasped. Spikes of lightning were flowing from her into each and every one of them. This was why it hurt. They were draining her. She didn't know how she knew. She just did. They weren't channeling her magic. They were stealing it!

They'd betrayed her. Lied to her. The shock was painful, for she'd trusted them without question. And her aunt. How could she do this to her own niece? Did mom know this was the type of person Melissa was all along, and that's why they weren't close? Had everything been one massive lie? It had to have been, for this was clearly their plan all along, and Melissa had done whatever was necessary to get Georgia's cooperation.

This spell would mean the death of the hunter. And her. She felt so foolish for not asking more questions, for not insisting on being more involved. She'd let them fob her off. She was new to witchcraft and had believed she wouldn't understand, that it was too advanced and intricate for her. *All a lie*. The truth was they needed her power, all of it, and would stop at nothing to get it. The truth hurt.

She tried to stop it, to stop the flow, but it was impossible—it was streaming from her fast, and she was already starting to feel weak. It was hard to breathe; it was like the glowing light was suffocating her. She sucked in a gulping breath. Panic set in. Her heart was pounding in her chest, but she felt like her blood wasn't moving. Her hands and feet felt frozen, unable to move.

A movement outside the witches' circle caught her eye. No one should be here. The building was warded so that people didn't notice its existence. She squinted, trying to make out the figure that was silently approaching, moving from shadow to shadow to avoid detection.

Pain surged through her, a scream ripping from her throat, her head tipping back as the electricity burnt her from the inside out. Oh, my god, this kept getting worse and worse. They were stealing her magic, which in turn was killing her. Again she didn't know how she knew, but some sense was telling her she needed to get the hell out of Dodge if she was going to survive this. She was panting, adjusting to the new level of pain, when she opened her eyes and saw him. Zak. Or, more correctly, the hunter.

He was behind her aunt and in his hand was her

dagger. The first blade. She watched, eyes widening in horror, expecting him to draw the blade across her aunt's throat. His eyes met hers, but she couldn't make out what he was thinking. Satisfaction? Hatred? Sorrow?

His arm raised, and the blade was speeding through the air. It hit her in the chest, buried deep. She gasped, looking down to see the carved handle protruding from her body, blood pooling around it and running down the front of her robe. In shock, she looked back up. He was there, watching, face unreadable. Confusion swirled through her mind. She'd trusted the witches, and all along, they had intended to sacrifice her to save themselves.

The betrayal stung but hadn't had a chance to sink in. And now the hunter had killed her, for surely she was dying. She fell to her knees, still watching him. A tear slipped down her cheek, and for a moment, his expression changed, a look of regret, which was quickly marked by indifference. She wanted to laugh out loud, for now, it was all making sense, but the knife in her chest stopped everything —her breathing, soon her heart.

She had powerful magic. The witches needed it and were prepared to kill her for it. And the hunter had told her many times that she was his ultimate weapon, only she'd never understood what he meant. But now...she did. For as she died, so the witches died with her. They were tied to her. She collapsed from her knees onto her side, her head hitting the concrete with a crack, but she didn't feel the pain. She watched as the witches in her line of vision toppled could hear them as they fell behind her. Like dominoes, she was the first to fall, and they followed. She could just make out Zak, unmoving, his eyes still on her. She'd thought he'd be smiling, gloating at his victory. Instead, his face was a stony mask. She tried to focus on it, but darkness was blurring the edges of her vision. A burst of panic shot through her, making her body twitch. She'd never see Zak again. Her Zak, the man who loved her, not this version of Zak who had hijacked his body and didn't give a damn about her.

Skye. Blood gurgled from her mouth when she tried to speak, to beg him not to hurt her sister. Skye wasn't a witch. Georgia knew it now. Her aunt tricked them, lying to them to get Georgia's cooperation. Surely the hunter could sense that Skye wasn't a witch, that there was no need to kill her, despite the family connection.

She was cold. It was freezing on the rooftop, and she shivered. It had gotten dark; she couldn't see anymore. The wetness in her mouth stopped the air, and she tried to spit it out, but her muscles wouldn't work, and all she could hear was a gurgling sound. She was tired. She'd just rest a minute, figure out the rest later, for something was pulling at her mind...she had to do something...didn't she? But she was tired, so very tired.

She closed her eyes.

Her heart stopped.

CHAPTER TWENTY

Z ak groaned. He was lying on something hard. Hard, and unforgiving. Definitely not his bed. Opening his eyes, he took in the night sky above him, then turning his head, he frowned, not understanding what he saw.

Bodies. Bodies hidden by robes lay scattered before him, the scent of blood heavy in the air. He lay for a moment, gathering his wits. The last thing he remembered was the dream walk with Georgia. Her suspicion that it wasn't really him. Now it made sense. The hunter had taken over his body; that's why she'd been wary and suspicious. He could only guess that the hunter was done with him and had returned to his own body, releasing Zak from his hold.

A headache thrummed behind his eyes, and he squeezed the bridge of his nose, sending a wave of healing energy to take away the pain. Struggling to his feet, he glanced around. He was on the rooftop of a building, and judging by the taller buildings around, he surmised he was in a city. He turned back to the bodies, noticing they'd fallen in a circle. Then his eyes landed on the figure in the middle of the circle—red blood covering the front of her white dress, long dark hair with a pink streak fanning out around her head, blood slowly dripping from her parted lips to pool beneath her head.

"Georgia!" His yell echoed from the buildings surrounding them, bouncing it backward and forwards. He ran to her. Dropping to his knees, he cradled her head in his lap, fingers frantically searching for a pulse. Nothing.

"No, no, no. You can't be dead. No!" Her dagger protruded from the center of her chest. Wrapping his fingers around it, he eased it out, flinching at the squelching noise it made. Tossing it behind him, he clasped her face between his palms, gently shaking her.

"It missed your heart, sweetheart. Heal yourself." No response. He placed his hand over the wound and sent his healing energy into her, confused when her injury didn't heal. What had happened here? What had they done? He glanced around at the witches. All had fallen in the same direction, all had blood covering the center of their chests, yet the only weapon he could see was Georgia's dagger. Spying Melissa, he quickly moved to her and checked her pulse. Dead.

He froze, the truth sinking in, stopping his blood in his veins. He shook his head in denial. Georgia couldn't be dead. *No.* He refused to accept it, but knowing it to be true, returned to her, placed his lips against her bloodstained ones, and breathed into her. "Please don't leave me." His voice was a jagged whisper. "I love you. Don't go. Please." He gathered her limp body into his arms, clasped her head to his chest, and sat on the ground with her in his lap, rocking. He bit into his wrist and pressed it to her mouth, willing his blood into her body to heal her. Then he waited. She couldn't be gone. There had to be a way to save her. *Had to be.*

He didn't know how long he sat there before the buzzing of his phone penetrated the daze he was in. Fumbling for it, he finally got it out of his jacket pocket and to his ear, all the while cradling Georgia's unresponsive body against him.

"Zak?" It was Frank.

"Yeah." His voice came out a croak, and he cleared his throat.

"You okay? Something weird happened...like we've all just woken from a dream."

"Same." His voice wouldn't work, emotion tightening his throat. His cheeks felt wet, and he knew he was crying but couldn't bring himself to care. *She couldn't be gone.*

"Something's wrong." Frank knew. Shit, all the warriors probably knew. They had a connection to him; no doubt they could feel his pain. And Skye. She'd know. As if he'd summoned her, her voice came over the phone.

"Georgia?" she asked, her voice frantic.

"No," he choked out.

"What does that mean?" she screamed, her voice hurting his eardrums, but he didn't care.

"She's dead." The phone clattered to the ground. He could hear Frank talking, asking where he was, telling him they were coming, but he couldn't rouse himself. A numbness was settling in, and he let it, welcomed it. Feeling numb was preferable to the searing pain of losing her.

Scooping Georgia up, he headed inside. He didn't know where he was, what this building was, but he guessed if it belonged to the witches, it was warded to be hidden from the humans, and for now, it was the safest place for him. And Georgia. Pushing open the door, he carried her down the stairs. Okay, it was someone's apartment, probably belonging to one of the witches on the rooftop. Walking through the kitchen, through the living room, and into a hallway, he saw an open door at the end, and he headed toward it. A bedroom. He laid Georgia on the bed and brushed her hair back from her face. She was so pale. And cold.

He left in search of a bathroom. He returned with a damp cloth and towel and washed her face and neck, cleaning away the blood. Her blood. He stood, trembling as he looked down at her stained robe. It felt wrong seeing her in such an outfit. Cursing, he tore it from her, stripping her and tossing the torn bloody material on the floor. She was naked beneath it, but blood covered her almost from neck to toe. Scooping the robe up from the floor, he carried it out into the kitchen and shoved it in the bin. Rummaging in the cupboard, he found a bowl and filled it with warm water, then bathed her, removing every trace of blood, refilling the bowl several times until he was satisfied she was clean. But he couldn't remove the tear in her flesh, right between her breasts, where the blade had sliced into her. Why hadn't she healed?

Was it because it was the first blade? But it was bonded to her; it was her blood that had awakened it. It didn't seem right that it could take her life.

Sliding her beneath the covers, he tucked her in, trying to convince himself she was sleeping. Resting. Healing. She just needed time, then she'd come back to him. He sat with her, silent, the only sound of the ticking of a clock, except for the noise of traffic outside. That roused him. His warriors were coming.

Rousing himself, he searched the apartment. Pinned to the fridge was a flyer with notes on it. A flyer for The Black Cauldron, a new age shop on Azure Falls city fringe. Crossing to the windows, he peered outside. They were only a couple of stories up. He looked up and down the street but couldn't see any signs that indicated a shop named the Black Cauldron.

Stopping by Georgia's bed, he dropped a kiss on her cold forehead.

"I'll be back. I need to find out where we are so the warriors can help us. Help you."

Outside the apartment door was a small foyer and a set of stairs. He followed them down into a large room, stocked with candles, herbs, rocks, and gemstones. There were several pentagrams drawn in chalk on the floor. Across the room, another set of stairs. He followed those down. Bingo. Pushing through the door at the bottom, he stepped into a shop. A shop that sold everything a witch would ever need. This was the Black Cauldron. Crossing to the front door, he made sure it was locked, and the sign switched to closed. He didn't need any surprises. He went to pull out his phone, only to realize he didn't have it. It must still be on the rooftop where he dropped it.

Racing back up the stairs, he burst onto the rooftop, his eyes landing on the bodies of the witches. He'd have to do something about them. He couldn't assume the warding would hold with the witches dead. He had a few hours tops before the magic wore off. Spotting his phone, he scooped it up. Seventeen missed calls from Frank. Taking a deep breath, he dialed.

"What the fuck is going on?" Frank demanded, "Skye is hysterical. We've had to sedate her, and you know how hard it is to sedate a vampire."

"We're in Azure Falls, in an apartment above a store called The Black Cauldron."

"So Georgia is with you?"

"She is."

"Is she alive? Because Skye has been screaming that her sister is dead."

"I've been trying to heal her. It's not working." Zak's voice was flat. Emotionless.

"So...she's...?"

"Dead." Zak finished for him. "We need to bring her home. And we're going to have to do something about the ten other dead witches here."

"Ten? Holy shit. So the hunter took out the entire coven."

"Affirmative."

"Zak? I'm sorry about Georgia. The guys are all shook up. They, *we*, all loved her like a sister."

"Just get here." Zak hung up. He didn't want to hear words of sympathy. He didn't want to think that she was truly gone. He didn't want to entertain the idea that any of this was real, not for one second. Shoving the phone into his back pocket, he strode over to the closest witch and hauled her body over his shoulder, and carted her downstairs, laying her on the floor in the workshop beneath the apartment. He couldn't leave them out in view in case the wards wore off, and someone suddenly noticed a bunch of dead women on the rooftop.

After laying them out side by side and covering

them with sheets and towels, he returned to sit with Georgia.

"You know"—he pulled her hand out from beneath the covers and clasped it between his—"I pretty much fell in love with you the moment I laid eyes on you? You were so unimpressed with me, though." He laughed softly, "Pretty sure you told me to drop dead a time or two. And I totally messed up the night at the dance. When Veronica kissed me. And I was such a dickhead for not seeing she was setting it all up just to hurt you." He shook his head, memories playing like movies in his mind.

"Veronica knew what you didn't. That I loved you. That it wasn't just a physical thing, that you wouldn't be a one-night stand for me. That you changed my world. You completed me. I think that's what drove her to do what she did. Why she betrayed us all. If I could turn back time to that moment on the dance floor...well, I never would have been on the dance floor with her. It would be you, only you. And then, none of this would have happened. Marius wouldn't have risen. Skye wouldn't be turned. You wouldn't have been taken. None of it. We'd be at your farm, enjoying lazy breakfasts, hot nights. Skye would be running the shop, making dates, living life. You'd be weaving your own special brand of magic on your furniture. We'd be happy." He was silent for a moment, dreaming about the life they could have had, should have had. He looked into her face.

"I was going to marry you," he whispered, a tear escaping his flooded eyes. "I've got the ring. You would have hated it but secretly loved it because I know you that well. And I know you scoff at marriage, but I also know how much you hate it when the girls look at me, how chuffed you'd be that you were the one to take me off the market. Oh yeah. You'd have hated it and loved it." He chuckled and sniffed. Hours passed, and he continued to tell her stories of the future he'd planned for them. Never letting go of her hand. Still trying, so very hard, to believe that she hadn't gone, that she hadn't left him.

CHAPTER
TWENTY-ONE

The day passed, and night fell. The only light was from the lamp by the side of the bed, plunging the room into soft light and eerie shadows. His phone buzzed, and he picked it up from where he'd left it on the nightstand, Georgia's hand still clasped in his.

"Yeah?"

"We're here. Downstairs."

He hung up and slipped his hand from Georgia's, touching the back of it where it fell to the covers. Running his hand over his face, he made his way down to the store, where he could see his warriors waiting outside the window. They'd caught the first available flight to Azure Falls and then hired cars to transport them here. Unlocking the front door, he opened it and stood aside.

Skye barreled in first. Her sedation had obviously worn off. He could feel the nervous energy radiating from her. She threw herself into his arms and clutched him tightly. So tight he could barely breathe, but he didn't loosen her grip, just let an arm settle around her shoulders as he secured the front door with the other.

He nodded to the curtain at the back of the store, and the warriors headed toward it. He followed, Skye's hand clasped in his. Wordlessly they climbed the stairs, gathered around the apartment door, waiting for Zak. At the door, he released Skye, who looked forlorn. Dainton stepped up and wrapped his arm around her waist, dropping a kiss on the top of her head. She leaned into him, silent tears pouring down her cheeks.

Letting them into the apartment, Zak directed them to the living room.

"Make yourselves at home. Skye. Come with me." He held his hand out to her, and she stepped forward, clasped his hand, her body trembling. He led her down the passageway to the bedroom at the end. He stopped in the doorway, looked at Georgia, who lay in the bed, then back at Skye, who hadn't seen her sister yet. Letting go of Skye's hand, he placed his hand on the small of her back and ushered her inside.

"No." Skye's anguished whisper ripped through him, and he gritted his teeth, turning his gaze to the curtains he'd drawn across the window earlier.

"No, no, no." Rushing to her sister, Skye clasped the hand lying on the covers and raised it to her face, wetting Georgia's skin with her tears. "Georgie girl?" She held her breath, waiting for a response. When none was forthcoming, the wail that rent the air chilled him to the bone. Unable to bear witness to her pain, which was as great as his own, Zak turned away. He should comfort her, but it was all he could do to remain upright right now.

He returned to the living room. The warriors all had their heads bowed, sorrow thick in the air, so thick he almost choked on it.

"Did you bring vehicles?" he asked, clearing his throat.

"Three." Frank nodded.

"Good. We've got ten bodies to bury. I sure hope you've come up with a plan on where."

"Of course. There's a disused quarry a couple of hours drive from here. We can bury them there."

"Let's get moving," Cole said, jumping to his

feet. If they had something to do, something to occupy them, it would keep the pain and sorrow at bay. Zak understood. He'd been drowning in it all day and needed out, just for a moment, before he lay down next to Georgia and died right along with her.

"Follow me." Zak led them downstairs to the workshop where he'd laid out the witches.

"Jesus," Kyan said. "How did he manage this?"

"I'm not entirely sure, but I think they were all linked to Georgia. He only had to kill her to kill them all. They all have identical injuries in exactly the same place, and they appear to have died simultaneously. Yet, I only found one weapon, and it was in Georgia's chest." The last words were choked out, and he closed his eyes, pushing the memory down.

"Fuck me," Kyan cursed.

"Kyan, go down to the vehicles, get things ready, and make sure no one is about. We'll put four in the first car and three each in the other two. Put canvas down. We don't want to leave behind evidence."

"Got it." Kyan disappeared, his boots loud on the wooden steps as he thundered down them. They heard the shop bell ring as he let himself out.

Zak helped the others carry the bodies downstairs and stack them on top of each other in the back of the SUVs they'd hired. It wasn't ideal, but it was the best they could do. Ten dead women were sure to attract the local authorities, and they couldn't leave them on the rooftop to rot.

Returning to the bedroom, he stood in the doorway, heart breaking as Skye continued to beg, plead and cry for her sister to wake up. He told her he was going with the warriors, that they'd be gone for hours, but he doubted she heard him. His own heart broke all over again, he left, making sure to lock the shop door behind them.

It was dawn when they returned. Skye was lying on top of the covers, her body curled into Georgia's, her arm across her waist. The warriors shuffled in. Standing around the bed, they looked grimly at Skye, then Georgia. No one spoke. Skye eventually stirred and lifted herself off the bed. She dragged her hands through her hair and over her face and took a deep, shuddering breath.

"What now?" she asked no one in particular.

"We take her home," Zak replied. Making sure the sheet was wrapped securely around her body, Zak lifted Georgia into his arms. Her head fell back, exposing the long column of her neck, and her hair fell, the long strands almost reaching his knees. Her arm dangled, and Skye stepped forward, tucking it back, so it was resting against Zak's chest.

"Gather," was all Zak could manage through what felt like razor blades in his throat. His warriors circled around him, a hand on each other's shoulder, until the final link, Skye, put her hand on Zak's arm. He closed his eyes and teleported them back to Redmeadows. They appeared in the kitchen of his house. He knew the kitchen had been one of Georgia's favorite places, sitting at the breakfast bar, chatting with whoever happened to be in residence.

Skye was shaking again, and Dainton took her aside, sat her at the table, and prepared a mug of blood for her. Zak headed upstairs with Georgia, knowing his warriors were watching him with frowns on their faces, but he wasn't ready to let go. He couldn't bury her. Not yet.

In their bedroom, he stripped away the sheet wrapping her and slid her beneath the familiar covers of their bed. The one she'd made for him. He was exhausted, he hadn't slept in days, and he wanted to sleep one more time by her side. The room blurred as he slid in next to her, pulled her close, cringing at the coldness of her body. As tired as he was, he lay there, trying to make the moment last, trying to stop time so he didn't have to say goodbye, so that this wouldn't be the last time he lay by her side. His pillow wet from the silent tears sliding down his cheeks; he closed his eyes.

"I love you," he muttered, letting exhaustion take over. He slept.

"Come on!" She tugged at his sleeve, trying to wake him.

"Five more minutes, woman." He groaned, "I'm exhausted."

"No! Zak! Wake up! Now! I don't have much time." Georgia's sweet voice was insistent in his ear. His eyes sprung open—Georgia? Sitting up, he realized he wasn't in bed anymore. He wasn't even in his house anymore. They were in a field full of wildflowers, the sun was shining overhead, and he could hear the sounds of a stream nearby. Soft white fluffy clouds filled the sky. Georgia was kneeling by his side, shaking his arm.

"You're alive!" He wrapped her in his arms, and they tumbled backward onto the ground. She laughed, wrapping her arms around his neck and planting her mouth against his. Oh, her scent, the feel of her, it overwhelmed him. His nerve endings blazed at the sensation of her body plastered against his, the taste of her on his lips. He grew hard in his jeans, knew she felt it when she rocked against him. He groaned. Oh dear heavens, he'd never thought to feel that again.

"Wait." He broke their kiss, a frown pulling his brows together. "What's going on?"

"I would have thought that was obvious." She smiled her sultry smile and ran her fingers across his chest. "But you're right. As much as I want nothing more than to jump your bones, Zak Goodwin, we have more pressing matters to attend to." She jumped up, moving away from him in the tall grass. He got to his feet, his eyes raking over her. She was in tight jeans, boots, and a white tank, her hair dangling over her shoulder in a braid, that familiar splash of pink delighting him.

"You died!" It was almost accusing.

"Sort of."

"Explain." She began walking away. He hurried to her side and threaded his fingers with hers. She smiled.

"The witches betrayed me." Her voice was soft and laced with hurt.

"They what?"

"They said they needed to link with me and channel my magic, to make them stronger, said they needed the extra power for the spell they'd devised to kill the hunter. Only, they weren't channeling my magic. They were draining me. I was a sacrifice...for their spell."

"Holy. Shit."

"Yeah, I know, right? I didn't see that one coming either. Aunt Melissa sure had me fooled."

"I'm guessing the hunter got there before the witches could do the spell?"

"He did. He'd worked it out pretty much from the start. As usual, they'd underestimated him. He kept telling me I was his secret weapon. All he had to do was wait until they linked themselves to me, then kill me. Whoosh, the whole coven gone in one fell swoop."

"How did he know what the witches had planned? That they were going to link to you?"

Georgia shrugged. "Best guess, I suppose. I think he knew all along that they planned to sacrifice me. They didn't know that he had his own magic. I think he's a witch, or at least part witch. He definitely has magic."

"But you're here now, dream walking. So you can't be dead?"

"Not entirely. Remember when I inadvertently stabbed you with the dagger? And you died? But you came back when I removed the dagger?"

"Yeah?"

"Similar principle. The dagger is mine. I awakened it with my blood. You wear the ring that is linked to the dagger. You killed me with the dagger, but you also removed it."

"I didn't kill you!"

"It was your body, Zak. The hunter was controlling

you, I know, but in regards to the mystical properties of the dagger and the ring, it was you."

"Okay. I get it. Just, please don't say that I killed you." He ran a hand through his hair. *"But after you daggered me and removed it, I woke up, what, within hours? You've been...dead...for over two days now."*

"I think maybe it's because I'm a witch too? Something is anchoring me, preventing me from coming back."

"What?"

She shrugged. *"No clue. But the coven's grimoires could help. Can you get them? The witches were playing big; I bet they brought everything they needed to the ceremony where I died."*

He turned to her to assure her he'd turn the place inside out to find the answers they needed when her image glitzed and shimmered, like a television screen on the fritz. He could no longer feel her hand in his, and when he looked down, he could see right through her flesh.

"Georgia?"

"I can't maintain the dream walk for long. I'm on limited power here."

"Damn it!" He wanted longer with her, greedy for the sight of her, her touch, her taste.

"I love you." She smiled, her hand reaching for his

cheek, but he never felt it. She shimmered out of sight, gone.

"Georgia!" Suddenly awake and sitting up in bed, he looked down at her frozen body. "Georgia?" He touched her cheek, pulling his hand back when her flesh was still cold. He rubbed a weary hand up over his face and into his hair. It had been a dream walk, hadn't it? Not just a dream? Not just wishful thinking? He couldn't risk it. If she was trapped in some sort of spirit world, he had to help her.

The grimoires. She'd said to gather the witches' grimoires, see if they held any clue.

Ten minutes later, the conference room table was piled with ancient books. The grimoires.

Aston was at his computer, pulling up images. He called Zak over.

"I retrieved the material the first blade was wrapped in from Georgia's farm. I remembered she'd said it had some symbols or writing on it, but it was so faded she couldn't make it out."

"And? Have you found something?" Zak peered over his shoulder. On the screen an enlarged photo of what looked like leather, cracked and worn. Throughout the leather were symbols, faint but readable.

"Once I scanned it, I was able to do some photo

manipulation. This is the best I can get it, but we can see the symbols. I don't know what they mean yet, but I'd suggest we look for matching images in the grimoires."

"Sounds like a good place to start," Zak agreed. Cole, Kyan, and Frank were already seated at the table, a grimoire in front of each of them. Dainton appeared in the doorway, Skye's hand clasped in his.

"Now you're all here. I have news."

"What is it?" Skye rushed at him, but he held her back with a hand on her shoulder.

"Take a seat." He told her, waiting while Dainton pulled Skye away from him and shoved her into a chair. He took the seat opposite her. Standing at the head of the table, Zak looked at them all. Aston swiveled in his seat, eyes intent.

"Georgia dream walked last night." Zak paused, letting the words sink in.

"Are you sure it was a dream walk and not just a ... dream?" Frank said what everyone else was thinking.

"I'm sure. She's in a kind of spirit world."

"You think we can get her back?" Cole asked, brows raised. "Bring her back from the dead?"

"I do. She does. She's positive we'll find the

answers in the grimoires. The witches tricked her; they were using her as a sacrifice for their spell."

"What?" Skye's voice was high. Zak nodded at her grimly.

"When they linked to her to drain her magic, they were draining her life force. The hunter knew that if he killed Georgia during that process, it would kill them all."

He paused, letting that sink in.

"There's something else." They all looked back at him. "Take a deep breath. Tell me what you smell."

They all breathed in deeply through their noses, frowning but doing as instructed.

"Dust. Floor cleaner. A hint of blood."

"Do you smell a decomposing body?"

"No." One by one, they shook their heads.

"If Georgia were truly dead, her body would be decomposing by now."

"She's in a form of stasis." Aston swung back to his computer, fingers flying over the keyboard. "While in stasis, her body is an empty vessel, waiting for the return of her spirit...or soul if you prefer."

"Oh my God." Silent tears crept down Skye's cheeks, a weak smile tugged at her lips.

"Start searching those grimoires. Aston has

some images of the symbols you want to be looking for. I'm going to see if I can dream walk with Georgia again, see if she has any other clues for us."

He tried to hide the impatience thrumming through his body. They'd have one shot at this; they had to get it right. If they stuffed it up, Georgia could be lost to them forever.

Heading back upstairs, he lay down on top of the covers. Georgia lay tucked beneath the blankets. Her body was like ice now. It hurt to touch her. Like porcelain, her face was white, and he wondered if she was actually frozen.

Closing his eyes, he let the exhaustion that was still dogging his every step claim him.

"Hi there." Her glorious voice welcomed him. He opened his eyes to see they were in the same meadow as before. She was sitting by his side, knees drawn up, arms loosely wrapped around them, a yellow daisy dangling from her fingers.

"Hi." He sat up, reached over, and brushed her hair back from her shoulder, needing to touch her to assure himself she was real.

"I'm getting weaker." Her eyes were sad, and his heart clenched. As much as he wanted to pull her into his arms and kiss her until neither one of them could breathe, there was no time for that.

"Tell me what to look for. In the grimoires." He settled on holding her hand.

"From what I've seen and know about the coven, you won't find what you're looking for in one grimoire. The witches are good at hiding stuff. I'm not even sure you're looking for a spell because I've been through Aunt Melissa's grimoires a dozen times, and nothing stood out."

"We've got the symbols that were on the leather-wrapped around your dagger. We think they might give us some answers."

"The candles..." She shimmered in and out of view. She was fading— already.

"What?" He rose to his knees, facing her.

"The candles from the ceremony the night I died. They all had different symbols. Symbols I'd never—"

"Symbols she'd never seen before," he muttered, sitting up. Zak had left everything in place when he'd removed the witch's bodies, hadn't thought any of their paraphernalia was important. The symbols were vital; they were basically the witches' language.

Standing, he closed his eyes and was transported back to the rooftop in Azure Falls. It was deserted; the wards still held. Crossing to the pentagram, he stopped, eyeing the bloodstains all around it. The witches had got more than they bargained for this time.

He gathered the candles that still sat in ten spots around the pentagram. Five red, five black. Georgia was right—the symbols printed on them were all different. Arms laden with candles, he teleported back to the conference room, startling his warriors.

"What you got there, boss?" Kyan asked, nodding at the candles Zak had dropped onto the table.

"Candles from the ceremony. Georgia said the symbols were something she hadn't seen before."

"Let me see." Aston came over with a digital camera and began snapping photos of each symbol.

"I'll run them through my database, see if anything turns up."

"She also said that the witches were good at hiding stuff, that the answers we seek are probably split between the grimoires. And that it might not be a spell."

"It would make sense that the witches split the information we're looking for." Skye nodded. "But if it isn't a spell, what is it?"

"She doesn't know. She can't hold the dream walk for long." Zak pulled a grimoire in front of him and began flicking through the pages. They had to find a match for the symbols; he was convinced that was the key.

An hour passed in silence, the only sound in the room pages being turned and Aston's fingers clicking on the keyboard.

"Check. This. Out." Jumping to his feet, Aston faced the room, excitement lighting up his face.

"You've found something?" Zak was by his side in an instant.

"Fuck yeah! The symbols on the candles? They're a match for the cloth the dagger was wrapped in. Three of the symbols are upside down. I'm not sure what that means, or if it was an error on the witches' behalf when they were creating them, but look!"

On his screen were the individual symbols from each candle, overlaid onto the ancient text from the dagger.

"These tell us something. A story. A spell. I don't know yet, but they're telling us something. Now we need to find out what."

"We need to find the meaning behind each symbol."

"*Babe.*" *Zak wrapped Georgia in his arms, breathing in her scent.*

"*You've found something?" she murmured into his chest, her arms wrapped tight around him.*

"*Yes. It's taken five long days, but we've got it. You're right, the witches hid it, but Aston is a fucking whizz at decrypting puzzles.*"

"*Tell me quick. I don't have much time." She pulled away, her eyes searching his face. Settling his hands on her shoulders, he spoke slowly and clearly. "You need to repeat these words—they will take you to the hunter.*"

"*To the hunter?*"

"*He's the key.*"

"*I must destroy him? But how?*"

"*The grimoires don't say, exactly. They do say you'll know what to do when you enter the Hunter's Lair.*"

She blew out a sigh. "Okay, what do I need to say?"

"*Repeat after me: Goddess of light, guide me in this quest...*"

"*Goddess of light, guide me in this quest.*"

"*Deliver me to my spirit, help me defeat the beast.*"

"*Deliver me to my spirit, help me defeat the beast.*"

The field they were standing in began to spin, faster and faster. Zak was ripped away, sucked back to his body, she hoped. The wind tore and pulled at her; lights flashed and surrounded her in a riot of color. Her stomach churned as her legs were pulled out from under her, and she was whipped up into the air, tumbling head over heels, arms and legs flailing. She screamed, the sound lost in the storm that spun her out of control.

Georgia cautiously opened her eyes. The storm that had pulled her through the spirit world had stopped, and it was eerily silent. She was no longer in the field filled with flowers but in a dusty room. A single light bulb swung from the ceiling, its yellow light barely reaching the corners. What it did illuminate stole her breath. Three tall bookcases stood in the center of the room, each shelf lined with glowing jars in a rainbow of colors. They were beautiful.

Stepping forward, she examined the jars, peering to see what was inside. The colors were like mist, and some of them sparkled as if they had glitter trapped inside. She took one down, blew the dust off the lid. It had a symbol on the lid, familiar. She bet Aston would know what it meant now that he'd gotten a handle on the witches' language. Zak had told her she'd know what to do when she got here, and instinct was telling her she had to open the jars. Grabbing the lid, she twisted. Nothing. Damn. The symbol must be sealing it shut.

Tapping a finger to her lips, she prowled along

the shelves, looking at all the jars. There had to be hundreds. Were these the spirits of the witches the hunter had killed? There were no labels, no convenient names or dates, just the swirling, colorful mists. On the last shelf stood a jar with no dust. Inside was not only mist but glitter and what looked like fireworks, tiny, miniature fireworks. The mist was multi-colored, changing from red to purple to green to blue, constantly moving and changing. It was mesmerizing and beautiful. *It was her*. Holding the jar in her hand, she could feel the mist trying to break through the glass to get to her, to reconnect. She tried the lid, but of course, it didn't budge.

"Okay. This is going to be messy, but it's the most efficient way I can think of to do this."

Moving behind the last bookshelf, she braced her hands against it and pushed. Slowly it tipped forward. Jars slid off the shelves and shattered on the floor, the mists escaping and whirling around the room. The frame hit the one in front, and that too began to topple. More jars smashed, and the final shelf toppled, coming to rest against the wall.

The floor was a mess of broken glass, but the room was a riot of colorful, glittering mists. Her spirit found her. She sucked in a deep breath as she felt it breach her skin and sink into her bones, flooding her body with power and energy. There was a loud clap, like thunder, knocking her off her feet and onto her ass. *Ouch.*

"Oh my God," she breathed, running her hands over her suddenly naked body. "I'm back. I'm back in my body. Jesus, Zak, you could have fucking dressed me!" A clatter at her feet had her looking down. Her dagger. The first blade.

Scrambling back to her feet, she pulled a sliver of glass from the bottom of her foot, not feeling the sting but smiling in delight as her body instantly healed itself. Looking down, she watched as the knife wound in the center of her chest closed. Oh yeah, she was back and ready to kick some hunter ass!

The door flung open, smacking into the wall with a crunch. Framed in the doorway was the hunter. This was the first time she'd seen him—in his own body. He was big, massive broad shoulders and chest, towering over six and a half feet. His body was muscled, built for battle, and covered in dark tattoos. Tattoos that looked similar to the markings the witches had been using. His head was bald, as was his face, with no signs of a five o'clock shadow. His green eyes were frowning, and he was naked.

"Surprise!" Georgia greeted in a singsong voice.

Before he could take a step toward her, the mist swirling in the room picked up speed, creating a whirlwind. The colors were unique and mesmerizing. Georgia watched, unable to drag her eyes away as they continued to pick up movement and drift toward her. Her body hummed, every cell firing, sparks sizzling through her veins, yet it wasn't painful. It was welcoming. Tipping back her head, she spread her arms wide and smiled. It was like bathing in a waterfall of magic. The mist enveloped her, hiding her from view, and then with another thunderclap, it was gone. This time she held her balance, the power of hundreds of witches running through her body—their spirits had moved on, having no bodies to return to, but they'd left her with their magic.

"Clever girl. You figured it out." He remained in the doorway, casually leaning against the frame, not embarrassed by his nudity.

"With a little help," Georgia acknowledged, tossing the dagger in her hand, twirling it through the air to expertly catch it again, all the while not taking her eyes off him. It was tempting to drop her eyes lower, to check out all of him, because, sweet mother of Mary, this guy was *built*. His thick muscly arms crossed over his chest, and she gulped, dragging her eyes back up to his face, only to discover *he* was checking *her* out.

She could feel the blush heat her cheeks as his eyes devoured her. But she stood her ground, refusing to cover herself.

"You're beautiful."

"It's not anything you haven't seen before. You know, when you were stealing Zak's memories, his body," she reminded him.

"But I'm not in his body, and these aren't his memories. This is me. My eyes. My body." He uncrossed his arms and straightened in the doorway, drawing attention to the magnificent male specimen that he undoubtedly was.

"Your murderous heart." She caved, glancing away, focusing on the peeling paint on the wall instead.

"It's not by choice. I've told you before."

"You have," she agreed, then shrugged, "So now what?"

"Either I destroy you, or you destroy me." His eyes held a sadness that tugged at her heart. She didn't want these feelings, this reluctance to creep in. He'd killed her, for fuck's sake. And he'd do it again. No matter that he hadn't wanted to, he'd done it anyway, had captured her spirit in a jar and left her on a dusty old shelf to rot for eternity. Righteous anger filled her voice.

"You killed me. Now it's my turn."

His lips twitched, trying to hide a smile. "Have at it, little witch."

"Don't call me that!" Anger flared through her, and before she knew it, the dagger had left her hand and was sailing through the air toward him. Oh crap. Why had she done that? Now he had her only weapon. Well, perhaps not her only weapon. Her fingers twitched, and she could feel the energy gathering. She had her magic. Her very powerful magic.

She was the one who gasped when the dagger found its target, sinking into his chest. He stood perfectly still in the doorway, making no effort to evade the blade, his eyes never leaving hers.

"What?" Her brows drew together in confusion. Why didn't he move? She knew him, knew he could have easily evaded the dagger, could have snatched it out of the air and thrown it back at her within a split second. Instead, he'd stood there and let her use him for target practice. Only she didn't need the practice. She'd mimicked the killing blow he'd delivered to her. Dead center in his chest.

He sank to his knees, eyes still on her. She

rushed toward him, unable to help herself, ignoring the broken glass cutting into her bare feet.

"Why didn't you fight?" she whispered, reaching his side, kneeling in front of him.

"Because I'm tired. Tired of it all. This isn't what I wanted, none of this." His eyes left hers to glance around the room, coming back to her, dimmed. He was fading and, heaven help her, she felt torn. She could save him. She had the power. Uncertain, she bit her lip, jumping when his hand landed on her leg.

"No. I know what you're thinking. You're a good person, not a killer; you want to save me. I don't deserve saving, Georgia. For everything that I've done, I deserve this. Don't think of it as killing me. Think of it as releasing me. Releasing me from the curse I've been under for eight hundred years. Do you think I never wanted to love and be loved in return? To have a home? A family? It's what I've always wanted, yet it was taken from me." Blood trickled from his lips, over his chin to mingle with the blood running down his chest.

His hand clasped hers, and she let him, tears wetting her cheeks. He'd been cursed. Turned into a hunter, forced to kill. Maybe they could find a way to break the spell that had him bound?

He was shaking his head at her.

"I don't want to be saved." He coughed, his blood spraying across her chest. She ignored it. "You gave me a taste of what it means to care. When I took your life"—he paused, coughing more, sucking in a painful breath—"it hurt me. A pain I'd never experienced before. Here." He pressed a trembling hand to his heart.

"Oh God," Georgia whispered, "let me save you. Let me help you. We can break the curse!" She clutched his hands. These weren't the words of a heartless killer. These were words of remorse, of caring.

"Sweet Georgia," he whispered, his voice weaker. "No cure. Only death can release me. And only you can kill me. The first witch."

"The first witch? What does that mean?"

"Every spell has a loophole. You're mine. You were awakened by the first blade. Magic cast by angels. Unbreakable. You're a prophecy that was foretold eons ago. I knew you'd pop up eventually, and here you are."

"I wasn't awakened by the dagger. I awoke it. And what does Zak's ring have to do with any of this?" She shook her head in confusion.

"The ring belongs to the protector. Whoever

wears it is destined to be by your side, to protect you from harm...until you come into your powers. Until then, you're vulnerable."

"I don't feel vulnerable now," she said. A ghost of a smile drifted across his pale face.

"You're not. You've got more power than you can ever imagine. You are a force to be reckoned with."

"I'm the first witch?" He nodded, coughing again, slumping toward her. "There's more..." His voice was so weak she could barely hear him. He collapsed into her arms, his weight driving them backward until he was a dead weight on top of her. She felt the handle of her dagger digging into her own chest and wriggled, so he fell to her side. She lay on the floor next to him, eyes flooding as she watched the light fading from his.

"More..." he whispered, beckoning slightly with his head. She moved in close, so her ear was next to his mouth, and listened, jaw-dropping open at his gurgled words. Pulling back, she frowned. Had she misheard?

"What? That can't be right!" She looked down at him, a gasp slipping from her throat. He'd gone. His open eyes were vacant, his jaw slack. Her tears fell on his face as she reached out and, with trembling fingers, closed his eyes.

"I'm sorry," she whispered. And she was. She wished with all her heart that it didn't have to be this way, that they'd had time to figure out how to save him, but he'd told her she was a prophecy that was coming true. There was no evading it. She was always meant to kill him. He'd known that she would escape the spirit world and come for him; she'd just surprised him with how quickly she'd done it.

Georgia rolled him onto his back and removed the dagger, shuddering as the blood dripped from the blade. Wiping her eyes with the back of her hand, she sucked in a deep breath, letting it out on a squeal when a swirling mist rose from his body. His mist was a midnight navy with sparks of white lights, like a starlit night. As the mist rose and swirled around her, she closed her eyes and welcomed it. She'd been right. He'd been a witch who'd been caught up in a battle he had no control over. The least she could do was accept his magic and let him live on with her, along with the witches whose lives he'd ended. A fleeting thought crossed her mind that maybe they'd reject him, not let his magic in, but she needn't have worried. The familiar hum and crackle intensified, the magic waterfall sensation flooded over her. Then the midnight mist seeped into her skin, into her bones and very fibers of her being.

His magic was different. Soothing and quiet. She liked to think he was at peace, that in some way, he felt he had made amends. The pain and sorrow she felt at his death were gone, replaced with a sense of destiny, of acceptance. It took a few minutes for the magic to settle. The other witch's magic was hyper, excited to be free. It still raged through her body, exploring and getting to know her. His magic was already settled, and his calmness spread to the others, and they slowly quieted too.

CHAPTER TWENTY-TWO

"Woman, you'll be the death of me." Zak sat on the end of the bed, watching her as she dried her hair, another towel precariously tied between her breasts. She'd nabbed one of the hunter's T-shirts and let herself out of the apartment he'd been staying in, able to see the wards that were now visible to her. She'd managed to get a call through to Zak, borrowing a phone from a woman on the street, and he'd teleported to her, bringing her home within seconds of the call. He'd been grilling her for answers ever since, but she refused to talk until she'd cleaned off the blood and dust and was dressed. She was still a little pissed he'd left her naked to face the hunter.

"Been there, done that." She grinned at him beneath the towel before flipping it up to wrap around her head.

"You take my breath away." His eyes darkened as they roved over her body.

"I thought you wanted to talk?" Her voice dropped to sexy phone operator level.

"I thought so too. Then you walked out looking like that." He stood, stalking toward her.

"I know. Maybe I'm not in the mood for talking myself. Maybe I'm in the mood for something else." She dropped the towel, her lips tilting in delight as he sucked in a breath.

"Oh yeah. In the mood for what?" He pulled his shirt over his head. Reaching for her, he dragged her flush against his body.

"Sex. Fucking. Making Love. Doing the dirty. Whatever you want to call it...I want it." She purred, stroking him through his jeans until he was rock hard.

"Christ, woman," he ground out, "I love it when you talk like that."

"I know you do." She dropped to her knees, unsnapped his jeans, and dragged them down his legs. He stepped out of them, kicking them away, then stood naked before her, erection level with her mouth. She snaked out her tongue and caressed him.

"This is better than dream walking sex," she whispered, taking him into her mouth.

"Yes," he ground out as his hips began to move involuntarily. Closing her lips around him, she sucked and pressed her tongue along the swollen vein on his shaft.

"Mother of God." He gasped, grabbing her hair and pulling away.

"You don't like?" She frowned, looking up at him, her lips shining with wetness.

"I like it too damn much, little witch. I'll come in two seconds if you keep that up!"

Pulling her to her feet, he rested his forehead against hers, his breathing labored. "I love it. I love your mouth on me. The magic in your tongue alone does my head in, but I need to touch you too, taste you. Fuck it, I just want to be inside you." He growled, threw her onto the bed, and followed her down. Pinning her hands above her head, he dropped his mouth to her neck, kissing, nibbling, licking his way lower to her breast.

"Leave your hands there," he commanded,

releasing her to cup her other breast in his hand and tease the nipple between his fingers as his teeth nipped and his mouth sucked at the other. She arched into him, little cries leaving her throat. Leaving her breasts in the capable hands of his fingers, he traveled lower, laving her stomach, hips, thighs. He nudged her legs open and settled between them, hands reluctantly leaving her breasts to skim down her sides, over her hips to slide beneath her and lift her to his mouth.

"Oh!" She let out a choked gasp as his tongue parted her folds and swept up in one long caress. Her hands tangled in the sheet above her head as she held on for dear life while his tongue did wonderful things.

"Stop," she whispered, clenching her legs against his head. He looked up at her.

"Am I hurting you, love?" He frowned in concern. She shook her head, face flushed.

"I need you inside me," she admitted. She relaxed her legs, releasing him, and he smiled, crawling up her body to settle against her, pushing into her slowly. She trembled beneath him, wrapping her legs around his waist to pull him deeper.

With each thrust, she arched up to meet him,

driving him wild until he was pounding into her relentlessly. Digging her nails into his back, she clamped her teeth into his shoulder, pulling his blood into her mouth. He roared, pumped harder, and returned her love bite, his fangs sinking into her neck and triggering her climax.

"I love you." He wrapped her in his arms and dropped kisses across her cheek to lightly nibble on her swollen lips.

"I love you too." Her voice hoarse from her screams, she blushed a little knowing the warriors would have heard them.

"Tell me. Everything. I need to know." His head dropped back on the pillow, and he pulled her in close, tucking her head in the hollow between his shoulder and neck. She dropped a kiss on his chest and explained everything. The witches betrayal, the hunter who had stolen their magic, how she'd broken the jars and the souls of the witches were released, moving on to the ever after, while their magic lived on in her. How the hunter had wanted to die, and his parting words to her.

"First witch?" Zak murmured. "What does that mean?"

"I asked the same thing. It means I'm the first of the next generation...of witches."

"The next generation? I'm still not following," Zak said.

"Well...this isn't confirmed...and I'm not sure it's true...but..." She hesitated. It sounded crazy even to her because it couldn't possibly be true.

"What is it?" He raised his head to look at her, concern in his eyes.

"The hunter told me I'm pregnant. That the child I'm carrying is the beginning of a new age of witches, and I'm the first witch."

"Pregnant? Sorry, sweetheart, not possible." He hugged her a little tighter. "I can't reproduce, and neither can you. There is zero chance you can be pregnant. Besides...even if there was the remotest possibility, I'd know it. We'd know it. We'd hear the heartbeat. Sense the change in your body. I'm not getting any of that."

"Zak? I think it might be true. I feel different. It could be all this magic, but, I don't know, something feels different. What if he's right?" She sat up, clutching the sheet to her chest and looking down at him, a frown drawing her brows together. "I'm not sure I'm good parent material. I drink way too much. I lose my temper way too often. And to be honest, I wasn't particularly sorry that when I became a vampire, I lost the ability to have kids. It took that decision away. But now?"

"Babe, you'd make a great mom. I promise you, you've got nothing to worry about. But seriously? You're a vampire." When she opened her mouth to protest, he held up a hand in acknowledgment. "Okay, okay, you're part vampire, part witch. Not human."

"But the witch part? Witches are human, Zak. They have children. And you're a hybrid too. Part angel. Clearly, angels can reproduce, or you wouldn't exist. What if the hybrid parts of us...?"

"Wait here." He cut her off. Sliding out of bed and pulling on his clothes, he disappeared, only to return minutes later holding a paper bag with the local chemist logo on it. He tossed it at her, and she caught it, clutching it to her chest.

Opening the bag, she looked inside, already knowing what it was. A pregnancy test. Zak pointed to the bathroom, and she obediently slid out of bed and ensconced herself in the bathroom. As she peed on the stick, her mind whirled. It couldn't be possible, shouldn't be possible, but what if? Stranger things had happened, right? She'd been a vampire. Now she was a vampire-witch hybrid. A super-powerful mega witch destined to birth a new line of witches. It was her prophecy. She was the reason the hunter was cursed.

Sitting the test on the counter, she flushed and washed her hands, eyeing herself critically in the mirror above the sink. She'd changed again. When she first became a vampire, her skin had a strange glow, her hair was super glossy and shiny, and her nipples and lips had turned a berry red. Now her skin was more human, sun-kissed like she was used to. Her hair maintained its shine, but her lips and nipples were pink again, the strong red color faded.

And she liked it. She finally admitted the truth. The vampire life wasn't for her, but with her witch bloodline, things were different. A little crazy, a little scary, but she felt...hopeful. She wasn't sure what being the first witch meant, what responsibilities it would lay at her door. Still, she was prepared to embrace them, for she finally felt at peace with the direction her life was headed. And if there was a baby? Well, she'd do whatever she could to be a good mom, the best she could be. It might mean reading a book or two on parenthood, for the thought of being responsible for a tiny human was equally terrifying as it was exciting – she knew nothing of babies, apart from they cried a lot and pooped a lot.

Her hand wandered to her abdomen, stroking softly across her belly. Could there really be a baby? Could a little Georgia or a little Zak be growing inside her? A slight grin tugged at her lips, and a zing of excitement traveled up her spine. She hoped so. Now that the seed had been planted, so to speak, she hoped it was true.

A knock on the door made her jump. "You okay in there?" Zak's voice was laced with concern.

"I'm fine."

"Can I come in?"

"Not yet. I just need a minute. Or three." She wanted to see the test results first. It was unfair, she knew, since it affected Zak, and he deserved to know if he was going to be a dad right along with her, but she just needed a second to absorb the news herself. She grabbed a dry towel and wrapped it around herself, covering her nakedness. This felt like a conversation that didn't need the distraction of naked flesh.

Finally, she turned to the test sitting on the counter, picked it up, and looked.

"Oh."

"Georgia?"

She opened the door and held the stick out to Zak. His eyes held hers for a moment before dropping to the plastic wand she held in her hand. On display in all its digital glory was one word.

Pregnant.

THE END...for now

Want to find out what happens next for Zak and Georgia? Continue the story in book three, First Blood!

WHAT'S NEXT

More from Georgia, Zak, and the gang in **First Blood**.

www.JaneHinchey.com/awakening-series-first-blood

Afterword

Thank you for reading, if you enjoyed **First Witch**, please consider leaving a review.

If you'd like to find a complete list of my books, including series and reading order, please visit my website at:

www.JaneHinchey.com

Remember earlier I said I mostly wrote cozy mysteries now? Fear not, I have more urban fantasy books written under my pen name, **Zahra Stone**. You can check them out here:

www.ZahraStone.com

If you'd like to sign up to receive emails with the latest news, exclusive offers, and more, you can do that here:

www.JaneHinchey.com/subscribe

And finally, you're welcome to join my VIP reader's group here:

www.JaneHinchey.com/LittleDevils

Thank you so much for taking a chance and reading my book — I do this for you.

xoxo

Jane

About the Author

Jane Hinchey is an Aussie author who loves to write cozy mysteries with plenty of laughs and mayhem along the way — who says murder can't be fun? Her bestselling Ghost Detective series combines all of this into an intriguing melting pot of paranormal danger, fast-paced action, and plenty of tongue-in-cheek snarky humor.

Jane lives in the mortal realm with her non-paranormal man, two cats whose paranormal status is yet to be determined (she did catch them trying to open a portal in the kitchen that one time), and a turtle named Squirt (who is massive).

Sometimes, when the supernatural chaos calls for a different kind of story, she writes under the name Zahra Stone, where the characters you meet are as sexy as they are deadly.

Connect with Jane at:

Website and Newsletter: www.JaneHinchey.com
VIP Readers Group:
www.JaneHinchey.com/littledevils

 facebook.com/janehincheyauthor
bookbub.com/authors/janehinchey

Ingram Content Group UK Ltd.
Milton Keynes UK
UKHW011826010623
422734UK00001B/10

9 780994 600738